THE *End* OF A *Beginning*

THE *End* OF A *Beginning*

JOHN HENRY DAM

508 West 26th Street KEARNEY, NE 68848
402-819-3224
info@medialiteraryexcellence.com

I was a rodeo cowboy who never won the world or even close to it. Yes, I was injured on the job thus had to allow my injury to dictate events from that day forward.

Years earlier, I had attended college majoring in rodeo and girls with a minor in beer and study. Sadly, I own up to the fact that my interest was in that order. Pondering, then wishing I would have been capable of retaining the overabundance of intellectual worthiness that seemed to hold me captive at that point in time. Reflecting on these particular events from the past gives validity to the expression:

If wishes were horses, beggars would ride! ☺

Post life of a rodeo cowboy college student then a married man, I am quite pleased to say I am happily divorced without a home. It is beneficial to be so described for I haven't any grass to mow and needless to say I haven't a lawn to water. ☺ ☺

The last time I peered at my driver's license it portrayed me as fifty years old. A consequence I embrace not by choice rather circumstances from a scripted phase of life. Experiences in life have also given me a love of writing poetry. I will give you a sample so kindly be watching for a book of poems in the future!

In closing, I will leave any and all with this fact:

Success is possible only if there is hope and to have hope you must have a dream so consequently without a dream failure is inevitable.

A REAL COWBOY'S MISFORTUNE?

Author
John Henry Dam©2003

Beneficial Is the Look-But Crucial It Isn't
You Are Born A Cowboy-Like It or Not
A Gift at Birth-Blessed by God
Each Is Distinct but A Comparable Lot
They Treat Women as Ladies
An Honor Given-Deserving or Not
They Don't Waver When Committing to Favor
One's Problem Belongs to All
All Problems Belong to One
From Beginning to End They Are One
To Finish from Start
You Find One as One Hundred
Or One Hundred as One
Each One is Different but Alike the Whole
If You Ask Them for Help
and They
Will Bestowal!

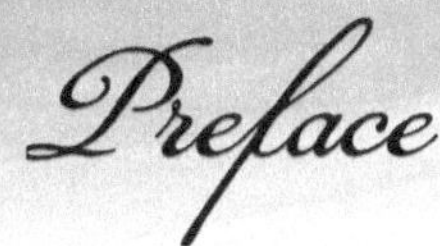

Preface

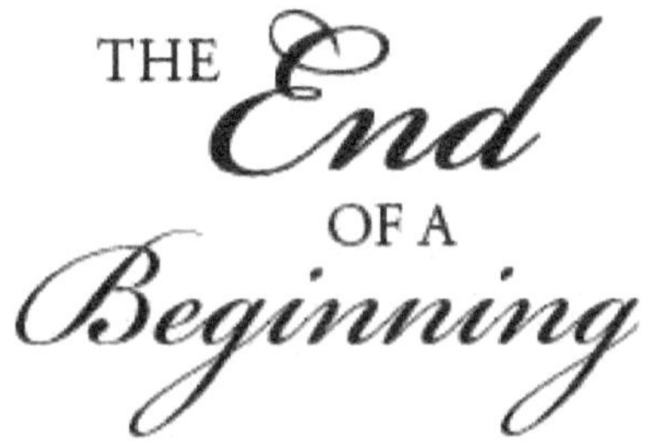

THE *End* OF A *Beginning*

A parable concerning love and integrity, infidelity and death, soon afterward devastation the forerunner for a new life. Revolving to show a fable of heart- wrenching determination. Rudy, being a man of substance and loyalty. Compassion his poorest tribute.

A Story illustrating:

For marriage, loyalty and truth are relative but quite sadly not simultaneous. This allegation indicating that conception at times misdirects happiness when commitment is not adhered to.

Demented but laughable, finding infidelity a seedling of joy? With discovery inducing devastation, birthing life after death.

Chapter 1

THE END OF A BEGINNING

Rudy was not a big man and small didn't fit the equation either. His portrayal of description included not being over- or underweight, and while these attributes did not contrast with others, he would be labeled simply as, just a normal, regular individual. Therefore, not retaining characteristics of distinction, the latter hasn't a place in dialogue. He wore his hair like that of our nation's finest, the military. He was reasonably good looking but nothing to write home and tell Mother about. His physical attributes be that as they may, were coupled with forthrightness and honesty, which were very important, expending an extraordinary quantity of energy to stay in his zone of distinction! These latter attributes were not necessarily endearing for him, seeming, he was living in an earlier generation when morality and one's word would define who and what you were. With that in mind, it could be suggested he had been born twenty years late. With that implied, Rudy managed to retain his integrity and honesty, which was an undertaking that seemed to be equaled by not a soul. Such a pragmatic description ascribes as worthwhile, in the usual, but for Rudy such credits were the grounds for his uninvited gullibility. So, regarding the previous forerunner, this would explain his ongoing character assassination. Understand, he continually attempted to visualize these traits in others and trust them as well, which did not result in his best interest!

The enthusiasm Rudy held captive was moving and enlightening yet heart- wrenching as the story goes.

YES! A positive conveyance Rudy exuded from time to time condoning satisfaction of present proceedings and future expectations, so by and large, Rudy reiterated this utterance time and again as his story unfolded about before then and then what was the future is presently the past. Bringing to subject a woman and her wondrous demeanor. She, being a subject of divine beauty with this description, breathtaking, and a matter of fact. Julie is her name, containing a tone unconsciously caressing. It's timbre seemingly fitting and having a resonance identical to her portrait, a jewel including her vocal rhythm, an Australian brogue, exceptional. He had met her at a convention in the South, and upon making her acquaintance, recognized immediately she was exceptional and a true example of a LADY. This, a term used to designate all too often gender rather than a woman of good breeding and morals as it should be. Rudy was taken with her at once he had said while recognizing, if possible, sooner would more likely be the case? Challenging, least I say was the past, therefore, Rudy had been etched with feelings of insecurities. His self-worth was lacking, for he had been hurt severely and was in the process, ongoing, of dissolving a union of many years, the cause no fault of his own.

A nose, Rudy's had been broken more times than he cares to remember. This extremity donned the motif resembling a snake trail. The design was imperative when referring to the multiple fisticuffs in which he had partaken. This was the derivative, or if you rather, the aftermath of more than a few physical altercations. A description that some call, character configuration, so nonetheless a part of his personality's portfolio. He just wouldn't be the same without that crooked nose!

Let us journey back to the beginning, where we locate the duration of misery being predominately the message and his dilemma history – over - or so implied. Inundated with decades of heart-wrenching anguish, if trading places with the devil we're an option Satan would have cried. Rudy's decline of self- esteem was exasperating, yet extremely understandable. At midpoint from the beginning, it was a horrific heartache, but totally a walk in the park when compared to the tumultuous outcome he was yet to face.

The sun's brilliancy being so dazzling it in due course destined him to seek a place to park. Upon spying a coveted location he sought, he simultaneously thought just right. Notable, it being out of the ordinary. His luck, in increments, seemed to be changing and for the best (YES)! Preserving his eyelids while pulling a few z's was the aftereffect or so he attempted. He accepted this certainty, he must be careful, while his luck seemingly was on an uphill trajectory, positive of this supposition he could not be. He could only presume so as not to misunderstand what seemed evident.

In five minutes, he was ready for bed. His bunk had become a stranger for lack of use and cast an allure of incontestable appeal. Rudy assumed his bed was going to be great and it was as expected. Finally, in bed his mind would race, therefore, he found difficulty accepting the truth of his atrocity being over or supposedly over. Rudy was truly thankful that his expectation of bed was not disappointing but delightfully fulfilling. Rudy's anticipation was to become an expected truth; his bed did not let him down. Drifting-consciousness exhausted. Calling to mind hitherto a parable entailing a relationship gone poorly. While in repose, his mind dissected time foregone! Even though lying in bed, mind running, Rudy was elated knowing this fable was at its end yet agitated and literally disturbed would best describe his fatigued character resulting from the disarray of prior events, then he dreamed as he slept.

As consequences have lain, they had caused an enormous amount of self- denigration induced from the foray of insensitivity encountered, then-thought- breeding a dilemma of disorderliness? Was it a dream or possibly a nightmare, this lasting occasion of influence? A fine line of difference but in all probability the latter. This duration was entangled, quite brief, but all in all its existence had been perpetually drawn out, it's passing. Illusive would best describe an attempt to isolate the problems as a result it was extremely difficult executing his will. The seconds seemed as days having only an illusory end or so it seemed. In turn, the days of precedence resemble months with year one vanishing. Mysterious was time elapsing, gone, and to what end, as well as wondering what the purpose was for this entourage and in what direction its dissipation would mandate. Rudy presumes possibly a delusion had transpired but the accumulative uncertainty of this episode suggests, conceivably an illusion had emerged. This making him question the aftermath and for what it's worth I fully understand!

The events of this continuance directing thought with the consistency of a beacon - a guiding light serving as an invaluable star to misdirected ships while voyaging at night a foggy sea.

That particular spring seemed everlasting; Rudy was striven to forget but futile is a description that would suffice best this struggle. Nonetheless, this in mind, he attempted to relay events of the interim that included leaving the employment of the second most monumental mistake he had ever been associated with from birth, the first being when he said "I do." ☹

The Lord watches and another fool he saw; bizarre his watch being timeless. The Almighty was attentive and consequently Rudy was sure this was what merited His fare-thee-well. In proximity of aforementioned time, he initiated a new work environment with his presence. A feedlot[1] being the locale of his employment.

In his earlier days, several feedlots had been his choice of occupation, preceding and succeeding marriage. Consequently, a stranger to this type of drudge he was not.

The feedlot of precedent is inclusive with the feedlots previously mentioned. The owner's memories were appeasing when called upon so relatively a challenge – not - him obtaining employment. Exemplary exceeding expectations when employed by another. For Rudy this was the rule not the exception and a rule that proved to be beneficial for him.

In part, his life had been punishing and recent segments should not be eliminated only accounted for. Ludicrous? Possibly in contrast but probably not.

A Woman's Dream

Introductory workweek he described as splendid to say the least. The

---

[1] *FEEDLOT: Where cattle are fed grain to prime weight then slaughtered and packaged into beef products, I.e., steaks, etc.*

day prior to Monday with Monday being his day off, Rudy journeyed to a friend, Matthew's, his locality a greater distance in the country. Matthew was quite tall and soft-spoken. Inclusive in this description of eloquence were long arms, long legs and a build of envy, having a refined and very muscular physique, although it was not inappropriately unsuitable. His physique, solid, long and lean complementing his movement of grace that included a tan resulting from hours in the sun.

Rudy suspected his genes to have a minute trace of Native American; nevertheless, Matthew would not remark if Rudy's supposition was pro or con. Him having a contagious smile seemingly and inundating his attention to the opposite gender. They were in awe of that smile, it being that of perfectly straight teeth and ivory in color. His smile spread from ear to ear, or so it seemed and positively endearing. This in turn complemented his mystical deep dark brown eyes and above his magnificent electric eyes was a full head of hair, dark brown hair and only a shade or two from being describe as black.

Matthew's persona attracted single and not so single reward seeking females with a want for self-satisfaction in their jeans. A character of integrity and morals – Matthew - absolutely never engaged in extracurricular activities with these married women or with any of the others or so it seemed for if he did, he never made mention of it. He just figured it was no one's business about his actions and plainly chose not to take a chance on hurting the reputation of another. This was Rudy's supposition but a knowledgeable one at that, or so he implied!

Matthew's curly hair may be more correctly described as wavy and seemed self-managing. A curl dangling over his forehead was enhancing to his already distinguished and handsome face. Entailing prominent cheekbones and a nose having a slight bend at the bridge, having been the recipient of a sucker punch coming from the depths of the dark while negotiating an alley one late night or early morning, whichever you prefer. He was not robbed, only hit once but his cognizance was nil and void for a spell. Hypothetically, Matthew assumed he was the mistaken recipient of the undesirable punch.

Matthew attempted to give the benefit of doubt to whomever

had hit him. He nourished a seedling of hesitancy when trying to believe his conclusion. A trait he learned from Rudy and one thing he had not mastered, for he himself would never do something so underhanded so consequently giving someone the benefit of a doubt pertaining to an incident of this variety was quite difficult.

On occasion while in Matthew's company, a feeling of inadequacy would befall Rudy. The inferiority - Rudy's - presumably, would not and is not difficult to understand. This, a feeling dispensed intermittently so actually a problem it was not or so Rudy insinuated.

After an interval, the local garbage truck driver found Matthew. Rudy was frantic, quite distraught upon the discovery of Matthew and did an admirable job of carefully arousing him. Jake the junk man as he was known managed to get Rudy's concern under control with Matthew's assurance that his look was far worse than was the case.

Matthew's nose was bleeding although not severely for the blood had clotted, and mostly, he was just a real mess resembling a victim in a Dracula movie who managed to escape being a fatality. Figure that!

The oncoming Sunday, a day Rudy will not forget, Matthew and Rudy went fishing catching a stringer of perch that happened to get lost one way or another and that would do for a good old-fashioned story. You know the one you refer to as "you should have seen the stringer that got away." That sounds kind of familiar, oh well, I will refrain from rubbing salt in that wound. ☺

The surprise generated by event occurrence is and was befuddling. Overcast in white and gloomy was the day when the snow made its appearance with a noticeable drop in temperature. Both Matthew and Rudy had resided in a rural area from birth, so uneasiness of the undesirable weather change was not part of this picture. The temperature change, while including the arrival of snow falling, concerned them not in the least but finding out later their apathy would be punishing.

They continued fishing for a much longer interval than should have been allowed, for time was not a concern but finally had to own up to the fact they were never going to catch what they had lost. Their friends would label them as getting skunked, which is okay Rudy said, because we know differently. Don't we? ☺

Choosing to leave earlier should have been exercised, this

alleviating the chance of potential victimization of a snowstorm that was inevitable. Bud, their friend, refused to let them make the beneficial decision of departing. Needless to say, this inaction turned out to haunt them.

Mother Nature, possessing a demeanor of no explanation, spoke her piece. Nonetheless, they blessed a bar they frequented time and again. An action that was next on their agenda for the late afternoon or evening. Rudy expressed playing pool was one of several things they had done that night and having countless good-hearted contests a little longer than necessary. For all practical purposes, Rudy's passion was playing this game of concentration and skill - pool - so needless to say Rudy had a jovial good time; for Matthew it amounted to nothing more than passing the time. Rudy, with conviction, couldn't recall Matthew even enjoying the game, although, if circumstances were customary and Rudy said they were whatever chosen by Matthew to indulge in he was a force to be reckoned with. Championing Matthew wasn't impossible but next to. Matthew shot a mean stick. (He was very good!) Having stayed entirely too long and having to depart with the arrival of closing time.

They were hungry!

Soon after exiting this house of suds, they patronized the local 24/7 restaurant with the privilege of their business. Shortly after arrival it became apparently urgent that the need of a bathroom would be necessary and immediately, if not sooner. Rudy trying to be cool on his stool so as not to arouse attention swaggered with much class towards where he knew the His and Her rooms were located. When passing the wall corner there was no one to be seen so instantly he made a mad dash for the room of choice. Rudy's luck never had been embraced with success, so consequently upon bursting into the room of deposits in a scramble for life, his life, he was sure, coming from within was the most eardrum scratching, screaming he had ever heard. It was only a minuscule away from bringing about a heart attack and almost relieved Rudy of his not so stable foundation. Matthew heard the commotion and rambled to, to check out the ado. Rudy's feelings were that of significant embarrassment and how or why he didn't know, but the need for the depository was alleviated. As usual, Matthew's appearance including his calm demeanor and smile of assurance settled the startled, bewildered female of concern to an issuance of understanding. Soon afterward an array of sympathy engulfed her when taking into consideration Rudy's sheepish look. Her displeasure subsided immediately!

Experiencing luck as a companion this late night or maybe early morning would best describe the time of day and that was good. Next, they made a decision to proceed homeward bound and did as planned. As it appeared, seemingly the snow had slowed and to this day Rudy expressed it is difficult determining if their friend Bud had affected their judgment or if the old girl who controlled the weather by nature, her name being Mother, had anything to do with it. Because … !

Rising early the next day, Monday morning, peering out a window, the view caused several moments of muttering obscenities at Mother Nature's temperament or lack thereof. Boy, oh boy, $@% Women! The two having experience judging snow and its depth from years of dealing with the weather concluded that an accumulative blanket of snow at least three feet deep give or take an inch or two was with what they were faced. Rudy and Matthew's surprise was minimal and in harmony to the scorn that had worked its way into their systems. This description labeling their unrest is just and then some!

Some people are lucky!

Accomplished at many things and inclusive of these many things would be to mention that Matthew was a cook equaled by Grandma only. They, or rather Matthew, proceeded to prepare breakfast more out of habit than a conscious decision of wanting something to eat. Previous day twenty-four seven indulging to excess the spirits they had partaken so incidentally attitudes were affected immensely.

The coffee was oh so gratifying Rudy had said and went on to say that mentioning the *other was completely moronic from his opinion anyway. The fact that Matthew didn't seem to be bothered by lack of sleep or having drank the well nearly dry really irritated Rudy. Some people have all the* *luck and Rudy wondered why the #$%@ he wasn't so lucky.*

Midmorning of this duration nearing sooner and Rudy pointed out much sooner than they desired. Surprisingly and odd too, time was dissolving with astonishing rapidity when they were wishing for pause. Conceivably, Father Time had his fingers in this along with Mother Nature and together Father and Mother were preparing Rudy's mind little by little teaching him to handle life's problems for the unknown that would occur in the future. This assumption may be inaccurate but I think hardly.

It was a pleasant thought with regards to the description of their wraps of cold weather being fresh toast warm lying by the furnace on the porch. A portrayal that would suffice and be encouraging when thinking of the abundance of effort needed to necessitate a completion of the job that faced the two friends. It was an effort for them and an effort nearly insurmountable and most trying for Rudy anyway. Matthew seemed not to be bothered, as by now it was expected from his prior portrait of personal design. Collecting energy within the boundaries of adequate amounts seemed to be an asset, which was nearly depleted. Success predetermines the effect of the culprit – dread - and of course then funneling the coveted asset – energy - in the appropriate direction. This agenda was nearly an impossible undertaking. The evildoer dread was causing displeasure so consequently was an aversion to accepting challenges of the day that was going to entail vigorous labor with little rest.

The time of feeling remorse had come to an end. With the finality of their apprehension, they donned their wraps and ever so gingerly stepped from a delightfully cozy porch. Briskness taking their breaths south[2] or so Rudy had said and implied the term brisk misstates the penetrating chill he was attempting to describe. Rudy and Matthew physically engrossed themselves with the job at hand. According to Rudy, it was colder than a well digger's bottom side in the middle of a March blizzard. He went on to explain so continued by saying that this was not an opinion of exaggeration, it was a truth leaving no room for debate. Undeniably this brash decision was in due time correct and final. After getting accustomed to the biting cold, Rudy and Matthew were led to an assessment of and accepting the certainty that complaining and crying would do no good. So consequently, their effort was as if they were possessed and on that account in passing located scoop shovels – two - then in rhythm, magically proceeded shoveling their passage from within their domain to freedom. With a newly discovered burst of intensity through the lengthy snow crammed driveway they strove. Striving to make a path wide enough to navigate vehicles through was the intention and such aspiration was met with success. Their work ethic was not dissimilar to the proverbial slave only comparable to.

Contemplating the past, Rudy visualizes young men – two - containing too much pride to benefit a healthy conclusion. The stamina needed and the muscle used was tremendous. A need, good or bad, remains to be seen and would be in the eyes of the beholder to be the judge rather it was to outlast the other more for self-satisfaction or self-worth, maybe both, than for the accomplishment of completing the job. (*They say Pride is a wonderful possession but their action brings about this concern, it being, the wonders if intelligence and the attribute pride are relative?*)

Finally interrupting a working mode of insanity, this insanity that if kept up may have been detrimental to a healthy conclusion. Therefore, ensuing was an earned break that was much needed. How they came to the realization or how it was bestowed who knows but they did and it was a deserving rest, for exhaustion was only moments away. A break much needed or come spring those who love them would for that reason be visiting their memories on Decoration Day.

Finishing a much needed and appreciated dinner, the fact they were TV dinners made not the slightest bit of difference. The dinner or if you prefer lunch was satisfying, very pleasing, the day after the previous day-night of brief sleep and many spirits. Relaxing an insignificant duration viewing television and Rudy emphasized it was good.

The aftereffect being to instill the realization of the huge monumental undertaking it would be returning to the job of scooping their outlet. (*Is it better to say down the driveway, or over the driveway? Up signifies North, and down explicitly means South, so over means, East or, West, doesn't it?)* Whatever the case is or isn't nonetheless it lay East and West. The last thirty yards seemed to be one hundred thirty yards. When the distance was achieved, they were striving for they had completed a piece of work that was mind- boggling. The number of short hours and minutes used to undertake the work was astounding to the mind. Baffling to Rudy why seemingly it took longer and more effort finishing the last thirty yards than completing the initial seventy- five yards! An illusion fatigue induced I explained to him, knowing actually it did not. Lord Almighty understanding eluded Rudy, nonetheless they completed this self-inscribed agenda without incident, withstanding a measurable amount of discontent and grumbling.

The happenings entailed next could have and I must add would have made a preacher's vocabulary be suspect. A county snowplow appeared and from the white of day the operator said, "Boys, stand aside. Let me widen that for you." Exasperation nearing eruption not unlike a volcano, Rudy never liked to be called a boy because at the time of twenty-one he looked like a boy of sixteen. Standing aside they did, implementing finishing touches on a job nearly finished came first. You know why, the story sitting playing Pitch.[2] Reminiscing at that moment with conversation in reference to the good old days. Telling anyone who would listen the tale of walking ten miles to school, snow five feet deep, uphill both directions, on easy days in nice weather. A story of likeliness when compared. I concur with their assessment.

The snow they had scooped, his gall, that operator, calling them boys. Rudy said he had tried to envision a couple of quote/unquote boys scooping that abundance of snow in time equivalence and was unable. "Boys," he had said. Is there no justice? What the case may or may not be consequently, Rudy and Matthew with impending need were the major attributes, I presume, allowing for Rudy's work arrival the following day! Apparently, it was necessary, massaging their egos, patting their own backs or something with regards to that. Them saying if they didn't indulge in this act of self-gratitude, who would? So the story goes! I surmise and question, will wonders ever cease, and the answer, I believe not likely!

Arriving home the following evening, Rudy saying it was good and second to nothing being there. He enjoyed a hot shower then into bed he tumbled. Rudy's conveying his predicament the next morning was comical and went something to the effect of this.

Rudy had awakened as customary before the alarm spoke its annoying piece. He then reached over systematically with intentions of switching it off, a habit and ritual developed so as not to allow its deafening spiel. He at this time then would emerge from the warmth of his nest. That morning, he attempted the customary feat and he did awaken before it screamed, but this morning he was adorned with failure. He did methodically reach for the off button and that was when it arrived. I am speaking of the intense pain that arrived like a nightmare in the night. He was overwhelmed. Then next came the buzzer. Rudy had said his alarm clock had a sound normally a little annoying, but such a description that morning would be a grandiose understatement. Rudy continued with a description to say it was a defining, piercing and an eardrum- shattering noise presumably not all that bad, but understand my friend Rudy was steadfast due to antics of snow removal the previous day. Lord, he was sore he explained and suggested it was an immense struggle finding success that morning. ☺ In accordance to his story, him abandoning bed was in itself a success and with this victory achieved he to shut off the alarm. He mentioned it was exhilarating instantly the silence and the temptation, a friend of pretension nearly convincing him to lie down for only a moment with intent of resting his eyes only for little while. Mentality, a virtue of common sense definitely must have prevailed for if he had so yielded being a pansy, which he was not, being there still would probably be the parable with a recital of may he rest in peace engraved into the memory. Beyond sore and tired he was nearly caved in, yet admission of exhaustion a sign of failure or a puss so not an option. (A Male Macho thing, you know.) Yea, right!

As the story unfolded before me, I could recognize the difficulty

---

3   *PITCH: A popular card game played for employment.*

facing Rudy while attempting to show any and all his worth as a man and that he could stand on his own two feet.

Too cold!

At that point in time, his car was not at his disposal so he had to suffice with only a motorcycle, a KT-250 dirt bike. Extraordinarily, his luck was malfunctioning. He had the bike parked inside the garage and that was good, although his concern was growing cautiously, as it hadn't been started for a couple of days. With a scenario with regards as such surely you are able to understand the apprehension coming to pass and his anxiety building.

Completion of the necessary safety checks and inspection of the gas and oil Rudy had found them satisfactory. He then immediately proceeded with preparations to start the steed of paint, metal and rubber. Rudy had informed me it did not have an electric start, only the good old-fashioned kick to start. Giving it a mighty kick, he said, and nothing happened. Rudy's surprise was insignificant for he only weighed a modest one hundred forty-five pounds, which did not equate too much force on the kick lever. Push come to shove and he kept trying. Finally a cough, a sputter, a choking and at last a ring, ning, ning, ning, ning, ning, ning, and it was running. Opening the door, he pushed it outside. It was cold, real cold, or was it what it seemed? Quickly his fear became reality and in minutes a realization the chill was genuine. He then mounted Katy. "Whoops," he said with a big old grin. "I mean my K T," then started his journey towards the feedlot. Discovering instantaneously, yes, it was as cold as first thought. Futuristic complaints of cold and heat while on horseback were nonexistent, not to rear that ugly head another time, not even once.

His ride, a frigid one but successful. Upon arrival, an older Mexican dude who Rudy said was probably older than dirt along with three young wet backs,[4] an offensive slang name given these men because they came to the US from Old Mexico. These men he spoke of as his partners in crime because they were all for one and one for all, subsequently they along with the Cowboy foreman greeted his return and its success.

Rudy voiced there were numbers of others employed there but day-to-day contact with them was minimal, hence, the wet backs of previous mention the major players with whom he worked.

Speaking Spanish was not an attribute acquired by Rudy and other than the foreman not one of them acquired the ability to speak English fluently. Needless to say, communicating with them was left to the imagination, quite challenging at times!

Is It Or Is It Not?

These fine fellows understood money, eating, quitting time and last but not least the P word. This symbol referring to the opposite sex. Rudy implied that he obtained knowledge of these expressions in Spanish rather quickly himself although he overlooked learning to speak Spanish fluently. ☺ Speculating about what is spoken of people learning languages from use and not books?

This curiosity leads to an inquiry of why people insinuate others learn dirty words first. For instance, the P word ☺, the oft-most desired entity in the possession of a female, whether she be pretty ugly, pretty skinny, pretty fat, black, brown, white, or just plain pretty. Why would normal people say it is dirty and refer to it as such? They of who speak of this entity are of all races, color, ages and religions. There was and are a few perverted females who have an acquired a taste for other females. That is all there is-is taste-and I believe that to be a fair assumption. Such an idea is without a doubt a sick doctrine, whether by choice or acquired by virtue of a grotesque genetic abnormality. Grotesque, maybe deformed would better describe their abnormality with more explicitness. Anyway, this behavior, right, wrong or indifferent explains their thought process and has a special revealing ring, unless you are one of "THEM"! ☺ ☺ ☺ ☺

That day Rudy says he'll never forget, unfortunately, he is unable to remember, which is typical of most days other than the abundance of snow accumulated. Therefore, difficult accomplishing necessary

---

4 *WETBACK: Slang referring to the Mexican people get to the USA illegally. Their backs became wet, as they swam the river to get to the USA without documentation.*

feats. Mr. Sunshine making an appearance in the days to come, melting the blanket of white and leaving an insurmountable amount of water. This profusion of water causing the fat animals to become bogged down in manure and/or mud holes.

When the mud holes finally dried, it was to the extent that respiratory problems became an obstacle. Wondering why constant adversity with Mother Nature and a continuing lesson of who is in charge. Solving one problem Rudy and his cohorts were inherently faced with another. Their problems were ending and never ending, moreover life goes on and to Rudy's surprise, it did!

With the continuance of life proceeding, his wife and children joined him and getting settled in his new home was fulfilling. A feeling of euphoria best describes an aura of sentiment as relayed to me. Was it fancy? Not by any stretch of the imagination, Rudy relayed, but it was his, hers or theirs however you wish to scrutinize this possession. It was warm and quite comfortable so they were proud of it. It was theirs, it was home, and to top it off, they were intensely exhilarated by thoughts of another child joining them. The two of them were filled with exuberant joy plus. This I reiterate because of the key anticipation shared. These common thoughts were that of another baby who would be joining them. This was a happening with much acclaim and was sure to bring much bliss.

Midsummer came and went. Rudy and his Mrs. were blessed with their arrival. A very much conservative description presenting Rudy's feelings would resemble extreme. Thrilled with the arrival of son number two maybe would suffice. Hell, how could Rudy not be, his new baby boy's appearance was a chip off the old block? Yes, sir, a chip off the old block, actually looking more like the block than the block did when the block was a chip! Imagine that!

A Miss Placed Memory

Having a memory problem as well and wishing for its return together with expectancy of a piece of mind Rudy so desired. Referring to a debilitating injury incurred while employed at this particular feedlot in question. A start to the beginning's end. This occurrence was in the autumn of that particular year.

That day, according to Rudy, started as customary or routine as any day at the office. The process of Riding pens[5] an everyday occurrence was being fulfilled and while doing the lower pens that so happened to be near the interstate curiosity wowed the interest of passing motorists. The tourists stopped along the freeway and removed themselves from their modes of transportation and walked to the fence line between the thoroughfare and the pens where the cowboys were in the process of checking for sick animals. Upon their arrival at the fence line they introduced themselves one and all therefore Rudy enlightened them with their identity as well. His colleagues and he himself, mostly himself, conversed with them for a while, remember other than Rudy his companions couldn't speak English fluently. The Mexican gents smiled and mostly nodded, not understanding anything being said to them nonetheless they wanted to be thought of as friendly and that they were.

Those cowboys were very careful, extremely careful not to allow their manner of speaking to go south. The intention they desired was not to offend them by the unnecessary use of profanity. This curriculum embodying or aspiring to these intentions sounds relatively simple, not a problem. Well, let me tell you, actually talk of this nature came with territory while doing your job. Seemingly when a guy's language deteriorated a mite it somehow it seemed to help. Anyway, Rudy was very careful. Yes, Ma'aming and No, Ma'aming, Yes, Sirring and No, Sirring, using pleases and thanks whenever possible. This wasn't theatrics; it is how he was and how he still is. He wanted them to feel honored to have made his acquaintance, so he did his best. Rudy wonders if his intentions were triumphant. No doubt they were.

These fine folks took Rudy's picture while astride his little horse, consequently, he proclaims that possibly when the pictures were developed, inevitably they would generate a few laughs and no doubt that they did. Recalling the intricacies correctly employs difficulty, he indicated. It seems as though they hailed from Canada but his memory was a tad foggy. This was the case as the story goes of his

---

5   *RIDING PENS: Checking pens for sick animals.*

misfortune. I suppose it's a miracle he would recall anything pertaining to this meeting, for within an hour an accident occurred with Rudy being the primary contender. He remembers absolutely nothing pertaining to his accident but has a recollection of incidences leading up to it.

The story continues with accordance of something like this:

Riding a young horse belonging to a saddle maker from the nearby town, and to be rewarded for his expertise in training this animal and others, the saddle maker would make him a saddle. Rudy swears everyone in the country that fancied him- or herself having the ability to ride a horse wanted a saddle made by this icon of saddle makers. Rudy said he did not use the term icon loosely for other saddle makers alike awed at his expertise and I know this to be a fact also.

There was a wait of one year to acquire a saddle from this man and that was after the initial order and that being if all went well. A most coveted item and Rudy had an inside track of obtaining one. This is giving validity to the cliché when said it's who you know to be an important item for achievement. Surely readers agree?

Annoyance becoming a factor I'll attempt not to be drawn from the explanation of Rudy's injury. To his recollection it was midmorning when the injury was incurred. Proceeding with removal of an ailing critter, Rudy's horse threw a fit and was involved in a horrendous accident. Astride a horse, young and tired, his intention going to the barn with or without Rudy, the intent - grain and rest. Young horses such as the like get tired much quicker than older ones. That being a fact a young animal is said to get barn soured. Simply, she wanted to quit work early. Rudy proceeded to remove a sick critter and was in the process of returning to remove another. This is when all hell broke loose. She reared to a walking position on her back legs. Lunging into another rider and at the same time hanging her front legs over the neck of the fellow rider's horse. She then slipped off, went to the ground and simply rolled over Rudy.

A precarious episode attributing to the air being squashed from within. This was the primary reason for his debilitation. A lack of oxygen, referred to as oxygen starvation to be precise. Funny in a strange way something taken for granted is so very important to one's well-being, OXYGEN! Ensuing was the injury and his fellow workers being the only ones present believed he'd gone to meet his Maker. Consequently, their actions were not advantageous to his condition for they covered him up. Pointing out again that was not a gainful thing to do on his behalf. It simply had to do with their beliefs. Breathing with his head uncovered he was not able, so needless to say this necessary feat was less than practicable when being covered. The dilemma facing his well-being is self-explanatory, I am sure, isn't it?

Rudy perceives from hearsay that it seemed to be a month of Sundays before the ambulance arrived, then getting him on board and soon afterward hauled their bottoms to the nearest hospital. The story portrays him to be overcome with convulsions. He said he is relatively certain it is an accurate conveyance of his being. The doctors baffled, having no response to revival attempts. Mystified would be a description of more correctness. In due course, they did the only thing making sense and that was to call for the Flight for Life chopper. Arriving shortly thereafter, Rudy was loaded then promptly hit the friendly skies hospital bound. With arrival at the airport, he was transferred from the great metal bird of rescue to an ambulance. Rudy had a cardiac arrest at the time of transit to the hospital. Arriving at the higher institution of care as quickly as traffic would allow and subsequently examining him with scrutiny were three doctors and two of three expressed in their somber but professional opinions Rudy was dead, or it would only be a matter of time. He was brain-dead, although Rudy had other ideas. Making an exit stage left not included in his noncommittal scheme. He was there, now he's here, good, bad or otherwise, will wonders ever cease?

Take Nothing For Granted!

His injury mostly from lack of oxygen initiated when that horse he was riding fell and rolled over Rudy. Resulting in a residency that entailed one-and-a-half months in the hospital. Was it a planned excursion? Hardly! Odd how unexpected events seem to put a crimp in a person's attainments!

The first several days of residency, Rudy was in a very deep coma. Physically there, mentally out to lunch. Days in passing Rudy gained consciousness. An instance he does not recall. Surprise should not be a part of this scenario when taking into consideration his description, pitiful to say the least. The aura of his visitor's empathy and sorrow was overwhelming!

Rudy's brother escorted Rudy's mother to his side. Poor lady, her description entailed being only a frog's hair away from going completely out of her stark raving mind. Rudy's brother, of whom he can't say enough good things about, did everything in his power to make it easier for their mom. Rudy thinks that God Bless the King might be appropriate for that scenario. Needless to say, wouldn't you say?

Surmising once he gained consciousness, it would have been downhill from there. Wrong! An uphill climb like Rudy had never been involved with, and he adds, will never ever be involved in again. Unless he's the caretaker not the care receiver. Making his point plainly clear is essential, for a quitter he is not. Death would be a more pleasing option than being induced into pandemonium resembling the ride that is close to being completed, Rudy explained.

Remembering significant parts that attributed to the extended stay in the house of ill repair are vague to him at best. Nonetheless strapped to a table of transit, they would move him to therapy. With arrival at the room of torture, they would remove him from the cart, lay him on the floor then attempt to get his legs under him. Comparison was a baby learning to crawl. With help, he would take one crawl forward, then one crawl sideways, one crawl backward and finally one crawl sideways again in the opposite direction from the first. The tactical stratagem's intention was to maneuver him into the original starting point. In days to come they mustered the challenge of Rudy crawling in the fashion of a figure eight. Taking an extreme amount of work and determination. Result entailing accomplishment of each and every feat challenging Rudy.

Moving on, one more tale first. Is boredom consuming you? I trust it is, I'm sorry! While in this particular room of incompetence there was a large ball with a handle. The handle similar to the handle on bareback rigging used when riding bareback bucking horses in rodeos. They requested him to set on this particular ball, hold on to the handle with one hand and balance himself. With his rodeo experience he thought this would be a relatively easy feat. Wrong! He sat on the ball, grabbed the handle with one hand and commenced to throw his free arm up like riding a bucking horse. Expecting you are able to imagine a docudrama being born. Throwing his free arm up and back imitating the action of a rodeo rider, he made mention that if having competed in rodeos for a hundred years never would he have been thrown to the ground with such astounding force or so he presumed! Throwing his arm up immediately tipping over backward and down went his body, hitting the ground, it had no give. A ball that didn't buck, a make-believe rodeo arena without soft dirt having indoor/outdoor carpet with cement beneath for a base. Understanding his despondency should not be difficult at this juncture when considering the description of one crippled cowboy. A situation and explanation, he hopes you to see the light of his predicament. At this time believing you now are seeing the true condition consuming Rudy. On a ten-point scale with ten being best he was probably a negative one million. Oh well, life goes on, and like he said, it did.

A Little Humor!

One time of many while a resident at this higher institute of care, his mother was pushing Rudy through the halls giving him a different view of life. Proceeding past a room while navigating the halls they ventured by an open door and peered in side. His mother explained there was a dude with his legs hoisted in the air, his arms in casts and lastly in traction. Rudy's mother informed him of his outpour of compassion. Surely it was his dad's feeling of compassion and defiantly his dad's expression of emotional identification when he said, and Rudy quotes, "Oh, that poor son-of-a-bitch." Rudy must have thought he was in pretty good shape for the shape he was in, or maybe the shape the dude of topic was in.

      Cowboy Mentality: The can-do attitude of a person no matter what the odds.

Another lighthearted incident that happened, Rudy isn't so proud of is this. Once upon a time he was in his room at the hospital, a Catholic hospital, so needless to say there were nuns coming and going quite often. One day, a nun came into Rudy's room, remembering this incident for sure he couldn't say. He presumes having been told a number of times about this incident it seems he does remember. Speaking of her and making a remark concerning her looks and I believe the observation went something like this. Remarking, "Damn, she's rough headed, there is no doubt why she has chosen her profession. Her face looks as though someone put out a fire with an ugly stick." Rudy made light of her look, a look that was beyond her direction. In the finality of it he was not proud of his less than sympathetic belief pertaining to her look or her appearance. Rudy just plain was not proud of having a less than sympathetic demeanor for a problem beyond her control. In defense of Rudy, he wasn't right either.

His dad mentioned previously, he fought a losing bout with cancer. He passed away before he was able to retire. He consumed entirely too much alcohol on a daily basis. Knowing the ways of his world he preached to Rudy not to do as he did but do as he said. Rudy listened for several years to his advice. The advice presented to him went as follows. Rudy said his dad said, "Don't do as I do, do as I say," and Rudy said he was here to guarantee you before his dad lost his health you listened to what he had to say regardless of personal preference and will wanting. You can take that one to the bank; it is a fact! Strange that Rudy had an attitude like he had, you know, a big heart with an incomprehensible amount of compassion. The reason partly was his being hurt so badly therefore not realizing the seriousness of his injury and thank God for small favors.

In prior years, Rudy had competed in rodeos and was somewhat better than the average Joe. He did quite well. The sport of rodeo is hard on one's body so while indulging in this type of activity he received many injuries but considered them as minor inconveniences knowing he just had to cowboy up, or simply put, tough it out until they got better. That is known as **"Cowboy Mentality,"**[6] a major contributor for the comeback to his present state of well- being. Good, bad or otherwise that is up to whomever is evaluating his recovery. Personally, Rudy actually believes he may not be as good as he once was but for sure he is as good once as he ever was! No doubt!

Chapter 2

THE TRIP HOME

While passing time, Rudy inferred time was not a concern, subsequently they vacated premises midmorning. They included his brother, sister-in-law and Rudy's subordinate, more properly known as his other half, Ellen. Subconsciously, he was predisposed and inadvertently referred to Ellen as sweet and little but stated a lie in his opinion, a horrific lie such as that would guarantee a one-way journey to a proposed destiny of no intentions. From force of habit he referred to her as sweet and was finding it difficult changing the habit. A habit and that is all it was, was a habit so decided he had better change his descriptive voice because he wouldn't want anyone to construe a misconception erroneous as that, thinking she was the sweet one when in all actuality he was. ☺

Furthermore, in that interim he was definitely the little one and reiterated the sweet one likewise. HO HUM, was his remark of indifference! Wanting someone to think differently was not in the realm of his intentions! She is what she was, anyone thinking sweet is opting for a rude awakening.

It was a two-and-a-half-hour ride to the house and naturally their appetites became subject of conversation, hunger became the issue. His brother, being the gentleman he was and is, offered to buy everyone dinner at a Mexican restaurant and Rudy added the food was "Muy Bueno!"

After finishing their meal, Rudy's brother paid for their feast. Then, not surprising at that point in time Rudy didn't walk well, which should be self- explanatory when considering the foray of problems with which he had been saddled. On that account when moving from point to point he staggered like a drunken sailor who hadn't taken a sober breath in a month of Sundays. With that in mind, he would expect all to understand when those dudes, two to be precise, raised their pointers and directed them his way, there was no doubt Rudy was object of conversation. He was quite embarrassed. In Rudy's mind, understand; there being only one thing to do about their insensitivity. Kicking the part of their anatomy, you know where the sun doesn't shine, so high into the air an alternative for earmuffs would have been their hip pockets. Instantaneously, Rudy, on the fight, so headed their direction. His intention giving them a lesson on sensitivity they would remember at their centennial birthdays. Rudy's brother had different ideas with advanced conception of the ensuing puzzle. Rudy's brother's immediate action leads Rudy to believe his brother thought he, Rudy, would get himself killed. Anyway, Rudy's brother wouldn't allow him to confront them. *(Good thing somebody had some common sense!)* Hells bells, whipping them would not have been a problem even if he was all by himself and Rudy supposed his brother theorized that would be his only option, with Rudy being as much help as a coffee cup full of water at a forest fire. What happened next was against Rudy's will. Traveling at the speed of light, nearly, feet barely touching the ground. Picking them up and putting them down going with one thing on his brother's mind, getting to the car and keeping Rudy shut up. With this the intention they arrived close to instantaneously at their car as a final result.

After boarding they embarked on the never-ending stretch of asphalt that pointed homeward. His brother asked him, "Hey, dumb head, haven't you got any sense or what?" Rudy replied, "No sense, only half cents." That plus the principles he claimed wouldn't get you a two-bit cup of coffee. His brother's lecture-rash-and he informed Rudy he'd better put a zipper on his mouth or someone would shut it for him for Rudy wasn't what he used to be *(Whatever that was)* so Rudy replied with, "I don't care." (Rather clever remark, don't you think? he asked)! ☺

Rudy's physical attributes were no longer only much shorter. The extent of his injury devastating and his knowledge stayed south, which Rudy expressed was probably a little better than worse. He and his family hadn't lived in their house long, regardless, it was good to be back, and where was his dog? Still, realization hadn't soaked in. A dog there wasn't and hadn't been for a couple of years. His post thoughts instilling the belief that he'd been fortunate his intellect had been absent, not at home.

The Agenda!

Shortly after returning home, Rudy contacted a friend who lived a hop, skip and a jump in the country. For a duration they visited then decided to start jogging to a midway point between respective residences. This they did do and at that time, for later that is, a video camera would have been good for laughs.

Rudy's way of going, captured on film would have been worthy of laughs. Putting his forward gear into high, he fell, his neck, he said, was nearly broken. He picked it out of the grass, brushed off and proceeded to the place of choice to meet. According to Rudy's description of his personal motivation, it was rather comical *(but not at that time)*. Spastic, has arms spinning around every which direction with him having to lean ahead when attempting to run. Thank God he said he didn't actually realize the extent of his injury. An astute awareness concerning the horrendous condition that plagued him was elusive.

Rudy would rise at six every morning and his friend and him would meet at their point of choice. Surprising? Hardly! The running got rather old quite fast, but they were determined to do this and this they did. The only days they missed were weather related. Their antics of rendezvous kept a timely continuance for approximately three months. Laying down on self-expected achievements there was not a chance. He had a plan and to fail was not included in the blueprint of success. At that time, Rudy initiated an effort entailing an attempt of resuming work at the feedlot. It worked tough, but he did it!

The impending Ex *(Referring to her as his better half like some, he did not. For good reason he never used that cliché, which you'll see why later on)* used to stroke her violin. She would tell him his injury was much harder on her and her family than him and his. Hello, she wasn't home then and never did she arrive!

What A Jerk!

Him commenting on the Ex's family led him to comment on the Ex's father. Rudy said in his informed and wary opinion this piece of work was and is the epitome of an amoral, apathetic piece of vomit to ever have had the misfortune of being acquainted with. Playing the big sugar daddy, when in all actuality he was nothing more than a pretense of a caring person. A moralistic facade- fitting-nearing bankruptcy and still playing God!

His Ex's father covets spotlight adornment and such an elaborate piece of works *(the Ex's father)* the mold, no doubt was destroyed when hatched.

An occasion, which inadvertently represents one of many episodes pertaining to her father *(Paul)*, is as follows. While in the backseat of Rudy's in-law's car, Rudy and Paul were riding, Rudy's Ex *(Ellen)* beside her mother *(Flo)* driving occupied the front seat. Paul quietly implied a falsehood to Rudy in a statement he had made. With hindsight in sighting foresight, if Rudy would have had half of his wherewithal about himself, jumping Paul's shit would have been choice of the moment. Paul being all shit, Rudy said he wouldn't have known where to jump first. Paul's remark was and I quote, "So your uncle never inherited any portion of his wealth." Rudy responded with an emphatic, "No, he did not. He is a self-made man." Paul, a pretense of a human being, said and I quote, "I know better than that." Rudy inquired of Paul how he knew better than that, and Paul said that he just knew. "Intelligent comeback," Rudy interjected and added he felt solidified in his initial belief of Paul. In Rudy's sixth sense, Paul was trying to berate his uncle with the intention of mentally destroying Rudy for Paul knew Rudy idolized his uncle.

Once A Jerk Always A Jerk!

Some more on this weasel Paul; the lesion Rudy mentioned time and again. An episode in Paul's basement, Paul and Rudy were alone, everyone had gone upstairs, a holiday the occasion. Having gotten financially inept, Paul was desperate to disencumber why this could happen to him. Not his fault, ask Paul, he'll tell you the same. That sets the next stage of theatrics, him informing Rudy it was he who was responsible for him going so deeply into debt to expand. Appeasing Rudy was the claimed rationale for his mistaken allotment of finances. Paul saying he thought Rudy wanted to come back to the family business. Emphatically, Rudy reiterated Paul was unable to admit failure, saying Paul's male macho self-imposed image dominates giving legitimacy to the expression, too dumb to be stupid.

Hard To Believe!

Next, Rudy referred to the feedlot to explain an episode that is funny but briefly close to being a tragedy. Rudy told of his responsibility for getting an old friend on board.[7] Adept at doctoring the sick cattle brought to the lot's hospital, the friend, Terry, was just an all- around nice guy. An experience that day, Rudy and Terry were riding pens, a task done daily checking for sick animals, a never-ending job so was never complete. Rudy and Terry spotted a sick critter so attempted to remove it. Piles of manure had been pushed up by a payloader[8] in the middle of the pen. The critter of meaning started to drift around one pile of manure so Rudy commenced to ride across the shallow end of the pile. His aim was getting in front of the animal to stop her retreat. This attributed to the end resulting in an episode Rudy will never forget because plainly and simply he shouldn't have done that. His mount[9] high centered on the manure, panicked and started to lunge frantically trying to withdraw from the pile. Rudy indicated it was necessary to point out his state of being. He was confident I was aware, but wasn't convinced that all others would be familiar with his state of affairs. You see, Rudy could hardly ride a horse that was behaving let alone one acting with such discord. Rudy attempted not to fall off, yet coming close to hitting the turf a dozen times or more

---

₇   *ON BOARD: A term referring to the hiring of an employee.*
₈   *PAYLOADER: A big tractor like loader used to push manure or dirt into a pile and other user of extreme force.*

in a matter of fifteen seconds. Lunging forward, Rudy tried to fall off to the rear, she set up, which kept him from falling off backwards then sucking back hard, which propelled him forward. He landed on her neck in front of the saddle horn. "Man, what a ride!" he said, adding if he lived to an infinite age he would never know how he stayed on or correctly stated, didn't fall off. Anyway, a ride he hasn't a desire to entertain again. He said, "No, never, not ever again." Rudy's embarrassment getting the best of him and actually it was no fault of his own but unable accept his inadequacies.

For a period, his temper had gotten the best of him and he called Terry every name in the book plus a few he invented, for good-hearted Terry was laughing so hard he almost fell off his horse. Visualizing this incident, it wouldn't be hard to understand the temper flare of Rudy but at the same time it can be easily understood Terry's ungovernable laughter that was simultaneous with Rudy's embarrassment.

⁹ *MOUNT: A slang name for the horse you ride.*

Chapter 3

TRYING TO BECOME NORMAL

Let's scrutinize normal, what it means to be normal. Normal and who is to decide if he, she, they, or it is normal? Days following, Rudy landed a job, temporary, hauling beets for a local farmer. Luck, good luck, seemed nonexistent yet seemingly a positive turn it had taken.

Driving trucks, an occupation new to Rudy it was not. Although Rudy had driven truck a considerable amount in his life, this was different. Which induces this reflection, is normal and different relative?

Rudy was required to drive a farm truck abreast a beet picker loading on the move. This would leave little or no room for error. This part the easy part and only somewhat of a problem. Tenacious was Rudy's demeanor, that in mind, difficulty encountered when dumping beets was immense, Rudy's persistency prevailed and his challenges were met with success.

Arriving at the beet dump and soon afterward would remove himself from the truck, a major success in itself. Then, as particular instances would allow, he would stabilize while clinging box side going with impending success, gaining access to the rear of the truck his intention. Feat met with success, at which time he then would release the chain securing the box's dump gate. This procedure necessary so when the hydraulic cylinders were extended to raise the box to a forty-five degree angle the end gate would allow deportation of the cargo. When Rudy's beets were expelled, the box cylinders were retracted leveling the box then latching the gate he would proceed back to the field of origination to repeat as often as possible during daylight hours. Normally and usually an agenda not difficult. Understand, walking on smooth flat surfaces was a mammoth achievement for him. So, an undertaking in regards to this, certainly it is not difficult understanding the obstacle facing Rudy. It should not be perplexing. Rudy's job lasting only a few short days at best so shortly he was in search of another job to challenge his inadequacies.

Time was and is a mysterious diversion, eluding the conscious observer. Seemingly it moved slowly, moving at a standstill pace would be a fair summation while disappearing without a trace then and now and Rudy having problems with understanding time deprivation!

With completion of hauling beets, an opportunity arose. An opening ascertained by his brother, driving a tanker truck hauling crude oil from the oil field to a pipeline. Recalling longevity of this second step in a mountain to climb, he was unable.

Ellen and Rudy's babies were Rudy's responsibility, so with an instinctual responsibility, he did not want them to go without, consequently eating once a day commonplace and always drinking water. Squandering money on frivolous items he did not and that is a fact! Back to the element of time, moving so slowly, expiring. Where did it go?

Brother Watches!

Rudy's brother, mentioned previously, once again answered a calling for him. Keeping eyes and ears peeled located a small business that Ellen and Rudy purchased. Receiving a significant amount of money due to Rudy's extensive injury, including capital received from the sale of their house sufficed for down payment. Rudy is thoroughly convinced, if knowledge of necessities thereof had been present to operate aforementioned business, probably another option would have been contrived. Twenty-four hours the training on how to and not to of that business then basically an entrepreneur on his own. Rudy and Ellen owned this business for approximately a year and a quarter. It was a success!

Starting this new short-lived career Rudy would arrive at work in late evening. Working as fast as possible yet moving with the similarity of a snail.

The next day attempted to head for bed by the middle of the day. His intentions were not always successful. A woman would join him alleviating a few duties consuming his attention. This was quite helpful allowing Rudy to do a number of other obligations necessitating his attention. She was good help and quite dependable. As for Rudy's luck it was no luck and she would decide to quit.

Rudy's luck seemed to be turning a little for the good. Just a little! His next helper was a dude not having punctuality in his vocabulary. It, a feat in itself this dude making his daily debut timely, a fashion necessary so consequently alleviating him of his employment duties became necessary. The good one came next, catching on extremely fast. To enforce the cliché, if it weren't for bad luck Rudy would have no luck, he landed a day job so went on his merry way. With his absence he recommended his brother as a replacement. Fair help he was but also accumulated no tenure.

Rudy's physical condition being what it was made everything he'd do a major, or better said a monumental feat, but giving up was not an option. Determination a persistent attitude, this rationale Rudy attributes for achieving success in the short stint of ownership. Completing everything himself faster in his dwindling days of ownership than with help when he first initiated ownership. Amazing? Not in the least! An amazing accomplishment yet it was to be expected so nothing exceptional or so Rudy led me to believe.

Day in, day out of this particular business got quite old with extreme rapidity for Rudy. Then the happenings that directed the immediate future, there is no excuse. Allowing *Rudy* to believe the White Night of Opportunity came knocking, when in all actuality, he confesses he should have known it to be the shadow of Satan. To explain this Rudy attempted. The shadow Rudy spoke of was Ellen's father. Boy oh boy, what an imbecile Rudy feels he himself was. Rudy explained; the shadow approached him with an idea of selling a successful business and moving back to the family business. The idea contributing to this impromptu was Paul thought it would be a great place to raise the kids. Manipulating Rudy's mind saying that he'd be able to get along even though he was a little short on knowledge and ability. Rudy feels this, an example showing significantly how brain-dead he actually was, but was dull- witted and took it hook, line and sinker and lives to regret it.

Upon locating a person with intentions to purchase, Rudy went to join Paul at his work. His intentions were to assist with the daily operations and this was the shadow's pretension also. When in all actuality a part of a plan in its premature stages setting up Rudy to give way and at the same time saving the shadow the big eradication by having someone to blame, blames!

Being raised around this type of work Rudy was accustomed to and a stranger he was not to expectations of a laborer. This self-impressed piece of work went out of his way attempting to show Rudy that he knew nothing of the expectations anticipated to be done, so on and so forth. Sometime nearing May's end, Ellen joined him. Furnished with a house or maybe better the remnants of a house they were expected to live in, being nothing short of a rattrap! In perspective from the present, Rudy sees a crippled and/or handicapped husband, father doing everything within his object of power, intent, fulfilling expectations of his goal therefore making an opportunity for his children. Also, obtaining a quality life for him and Ellen. At that time, he was convinced she loved him too, with joint goals one and the same. Unfortunately, this supposition was furthest from the truth, as readers will see later on.

Spring arrived and slowly dissipated. This period of hate and discontent, moving slowly in comparison, a minuet. In the late spring, they commenced to ready machinery for a summer of drudgery. Machinery included relics that should have been in an antique museum no doubt. Wore out old junk, so on and so forth.

Summer coming and going incidents many, nothing major, many minor of which are too numerous to mention. Prompting one's memory, Rudy was still handicapped, although get up and go had gotten much easier to get up and get going. Rudy's ins and outs, ups and downs and roundabout motivation was improving too. Even with his physical attributes steadily improving, he was a far cry from being (*NORMAL*.)☺ Did we decide what was meant by normal? I think not and we will not I expect.

Hard To Believe!

This exclamation next Rudy swears is true, but feels a hard time will be had by all believing this interjection.

He will swear on his father's grave, it is the truth. The cliché of swearing on his mother's grave he chooses not to use because she is still living, so consequently he is not inclined to rush her departure. Understanding this impasse, Rudy voiced that he was sure would not be a problem.

This piece of work and Rudy in an old beat-up jalopy pickup were heading for a secret fishing hole. He remembers the time of day to be in the early morning. Sun blinding traveling east when out of the blue Paul looked at Rudy and made an exhortation of why don't you try to screw Flo? Completely confused? Rudy was too. You read it right; Paul the shadow looked at Rudy and said, "Why don't you try to screw Flo?" Dumbfounded hardly would describe Rudy's surprise. Rudy feels he probably looked like he'd come right out of a cartoon. Looking at Paul and said, "Are you sick or what?" Paul replied, "Really, why don't you try to screw her?" At that time, Rudy told him to get real, and the subject was never broached again. To this day it is hard for Rudy to fathom him, the shadow suggesting such an atrocity! "Someone should have hanged his mother for giving birth to such a mental genetically deformed lowlife," Rudy finished!

More Proof!

Next, Rudy told of an instance monumentally not so significant after the last, but will indicate what a despicable lesion the shadow was and is. Driving a large vehicle, Rudy had raised the air seat so as to see the lay of the land much easier and also trying to find a position to take pressure off his kidneys. Rudy said the small of his back was worse than sore. With kidneys bothering him, he adjusted the air ride seat in an extended position, which was elevated to the maximum. The ground he had to negotiate was precarious at best, having holes in numerous locations easy to drop one or the other steering wheels in or possibly both. The elevation of the seat didn't seem to help and was definitely harder on his kidneys so next Rudy attempted to lower it but lo and behold it would not expel the air so wouldn't lower. He attempted to release the air from within the seat several times but it would not settle to a lower position. As luck would have it, he never was successful. It was stuck and would not descend.

No Heart!

Irate is the description best describing the shadow when gaining knowledge pertaining to Rudy's predicament and you would have assumed Rudy killed the shadow's mother. He instructed Rudy at that time not to ever get in that vehicle again. At least not until he grew up, referring to Rudy's size. Ignorance is not bliss, individuals making a statement of such accordance to someone in Rudy's condition is lower than a whale's belly resting on the ocean floor. Rudy knew then and he knows now he was and is a long ways from being (NORMAL.) Nonetheless, people with like similarities of Paul give an individual a shame complex having to claim a race of likeliness, to elaborate further is not essential. Paul's ways would give someone grounds for murder. Who could blame Rudy if he did? Rudy, a man of integrity, honesty and just a splendid, wonderfully nice guy and because of his worthy ways leaving himself open for misfortune.

Chapter 4

LEAVING THE PLACE OF HELL
ONCE AND FOR ALL!

Rudy surprised? Not in the least, but most everyone else was, well maybe, for sure Rudy wasn't, not at all. One day, Paul the pompous ingrate - the Shadow - approached Rudy with his dilemma. The time interval was the first of the year when the shadow enlightened Rudy that filing bankruptcy was his next option, it being an impasse beyond his control, unfortunately. Informing him as to this untimely circumstance it appeared his next option had been chosen for him. Owning up to the fact of financial ineptness, momentarily. Including pertinent information, it would be to Rudy's advantage to find employment elsewhere. Imagine that!

Mentally entertained propositions at these particular instances for Rudy were continuous. Presuming any and all to understand the insecure feelings that were slowly overriding and surely transpiring. In essence, they were dominating and in a debilitating way destroying his frail constitution. Rudy was amazed how sequence occurrences came to play and attempted explanation.

Sounds Like A Fact!

In Rudy's opinion, him coming from an established business to another business with less than a year-and-a-half of survival was a well thought out ploy on the part of the Shadow, including Ellen,

Rudy's future ex. I surmise this was a well thought out plan to disguise the events of the future, which were to include filing bankruptcy and making Rudy the fall guy. Rudy's state of financial success was progressing although making claims insinuating remarkable gains would be somewhat out of place. He was standing on his own and had planned to be there for an extended period of time. Unable to achieve employment doing most everything else he was knowledgeable about. He was at a considerable disadvantage but his tenacity was matchless. Remembering his handicap, or better said, his physical predicament, it is conceivably self-explanatory understanding his inadequacies. *(Mystifying to him and I also why a physical disability is referred to as HANDI-cap. Ludicrous the expression, a more accurate portrayal would be a cumbrous cap maybe better yet a CUMBI-cap. Reasoning for this scenario, a disability as such is anything but handy and this should be self-explanatory unless you are brain- dead, a Democrat, or liberal, which is unnecessary and direly verbose using those designations of description in the same breath!* Correct? ☺ !)

Why?

Rudy tried but had great difficulty putting forth reason for his dedication. A devotion with intentions possible but not probable, for Rudy it was impossible prior to his injury to please this self-impressed hunk of monkey dung, let alone after the tragedy. Rudy's question of how was he to do the impossible after the fact and I expect this is a question without an answer.

This example wholeheartedly shows how open to mind manipulation he was. Entertaining an idea of this magnitude, ludicrous and never should have been broached, relocating to the family business. Insurmountable love that a father and a husband have for his children, and also his wife, blinded an astute decision, consequently, reception for a piece of hell here on earth.

Digressing to the ploy of the Shadow. The most ingenious person staggering into a diverse delineation of this caliber, Rudy has never claimed to be but feels his versed knowledge of this ordeal is unerring. That in mind, he believes from his deepest heart-rending belief the shadow was apprised of what would transpire.

The opinion that was mentioned previously points towards Rudy's conviction. This an opinion, but eighty percent of it is an educated conclusion, the other twenty percent is sixth sense.

A caring, sincere person would not have enticed another to leave a successful business to join him when having less than a year-and-a-half of existence left before bankruptcy. Especially when that someone was his son-in- law. Rudy presumed the shadow to be forthright and sincere and as Rudy's story was relayed to me it sounded reasonable to presume him to be candid instead of so pretentious. The shadow's action, inclusive with his daughter, was a well thought out artifice to employ assistance without the assisting learned. This assumption - right or wrong - is knowledgeable in consideration. "There are always two or more opinions," Rudy said, "The wrong one and mine!" ☺

A Journey In Hell!

Making preparations for leaving! Rudy folks were not wealthy, although an uncle from the Sir side of his family was quite affluent. Having achieved prominence with spousal support by putting priorities in front of nonessential interests, such as smoking, alcoholic beverages and other amenities of no worth. This makes room for an assertion therefore opening the door to touch the idealization that Rudy's name, Sir name that is, was a major reason giving tribute to his accusation of Ellen's father's stratagem. A well-planned excursion and avoidance of proper knowledge relayed to the major contributor, Rudy. Keeping hush-hush was the shadow Paul, who was the instigator of this colossal contrivance, him not wanting anyone to recognize him as a loser. He failed in that aspect also. Rudy then attempted to explain his theory of what took place, it going something like this.

Doomed With Love

After they, they being Rudy, Ellen and the kids, moved to their new residence, Rudy landed a job driving a truck. Rudy's mother, a concerned loving mother, made a considerable amount of money available to them, earnest payment on a house of their choice was the intention. This act of good faith was a less-than- intelligent deed on her part considering Rudy was just founding a new job and knew not if success would be compliant or adversary. In her defense, it was not a lack of intelligence but plagued or accursed with an overabundance of motherly love.

Earlier intervals including single and married life Rudy had driven trucks substantially, but physically CUMBI-capped he was not. He now was physically challenged yet successful. So, it is needless to say as a career change it had been rewarding regardless of the consequences from aftermath of change.

Rudy's mother's financial portfolio would be best described as half empty rather than half full so it is plain to see she did not have an overabundance of capital, nevertheless she allowed them to borrow the requested resources. They were not able to achieve financing so the money that was laid down for worthy intent without choice was forfeited. They had made payments to Rudy's mother conceivably for one year, when out of the blue, Ellen, reasons known only to her, quit making payments. Having excuses of why, trying arduously to guide Rudy to the assumption that they shouldn't have to alleviate their unfortunate debt to his mother. Then, Ellen always was having more reasons than stripes on a zebra backing her misguided insight. At this time, Rudy was wishing a bottle of smart pills had been available and he being inspired to overdose. God willing, he then could have pulled his head out of that designated place with W's[10] on each side but apparently God wasn't willing so needless to say he was doomed with darkness for many days and weeks to come. Wishes are a waste of time, and to add validity this hypothesis is, if the latter were horses, beggars would ride. It appears this aforethought is forsaken and worthless.

They occupied this house of intended purchase for approximately one-and- a-half years. During the interim of their habitation, Mrs. Landlord contracted something or another and was in extremely poor health, which more than likely motivated their

---

[10]   *W's: Represent the hip pockets on Wrangler jeans.*

insensitivity to Rudy and Ellen's inability to obtain financing. As a result, the means to an end was not by their choice but chosen for them. The end Rudy spoke of was them forfeiting the dollars they had been credited with for earnest money. Mrs. Landlord passed away, which leads me to the question of why doesn't something of similar nature happen to those who actually deserve it instead of someone like her at a time of rearing young children? Baffling to say the least. Rudy just doesn't get it. Another point of maybe being mentally inept? Maybe … maybe not!

From early spring till early fall, Rudy had driven a truck for a nice sort of a guy. This interval of employment getting his proverbial you know what together was a tough time of trials and tribulations, some menial and some not so menial. Again, contributing to cowboy mentality, his conjecture for having the staying power to frown and bare it. Rudy would add that he did and he is extremely proud of it. A quitter he was not, so he reiterated by saying another time he was very proud of his accomplishments.

Early in the fall, a blessing was bestowed. It, being an opportunity to obtain a truck of his own. Blessing may be a little strong and probably is if what came to pass is taken into consideration. Regardless of the future to come, which Rudy new nothing of as no one else did, thought he himself to be a lucky man. Him possessing an insurmountable love of his little big offsprings and Ellen whom he thought loved him as he loved her. Topping it off, he had a brand- new truck! Life at times was good! YES! YES! YES!

Curiously peering back, Rudy wonders if common sense or mental awareness had finally returned tired of being south. An accurate description of himself would be loyal, conscientious, inferior and determined. The determination of which he speaks is also the fuel that powered his inability to pull his head out of the spot and see the light.

Preoccupied and so unaware to the nth degree when perception is considered. There is a saying that exemplifies his actions and I can't put a finger on who said it but goes something to this effect: *No blinder than those who will not see.* This would be an accurate portrayal and may suffice as an example constituting a belief relating to the following. The post opinion of not having a notion that made him question evidence that was unmistakable when Ellen came up pregnant and Rudy trucking so damn hard, he could barely keep his eyes open. Red lights and flashing signals making him aware of her extra marital activities were there, but Rudy says he was too damn stupid to get it. She forewarned him of her intentions, an act unthinkable to her he thought, but not! Her intention was an abortion and what's more she got it not just once but three times that Rudy was knowledgeable of and probably more times he was not aware of! Perplexing to him to say the least.

She beholds two personalities different as night and day. One sweet, the other menacing and vengeful. If looks could kill, Rudy infers he would be history. Mentioning the split personality deliberately, the intention is showing how he was manipulated into escorting her to the doctor to have her day of attention the first time, well as far as Rudy knew it was the first time!

While at the doctor's office, she initialized a put- down, Rudy being the recipient. Ridicule massive! Her objective to belittle Rudy and successful she was. Inferring the fault was his and only his! It was **Possible** but not **Probable,** he suspects, hell he shouldn't have had sex with her **both times that quarter.** Give me a break, he had asked and went on to voice that in his opinion if she had as many stray penises sticking out of her as she has had stuck in her she would make a porcupine look bald. ☺ She is a harlot who gives the term liar a new definition. Her intentions were quite devious. These intentions evoking disingenuous scorn in Rudy's direction times three. Old hat, being a veteran of what was to transpire transported herself the latter times for these special days of attention. Rudy, looking at himself, felt dumb and is sad to admit that. Amazing how love and loyalty will cloud the true picture. Figure it out – Duh - should have been Rudy's first and last names! Only kidding.

Love and loyalty the most wonderful emotions the world has to offer yet contributing to more financial ruination, broken hearts and once in a while the detonator behind murder. Feeling used, abused and lonesome, Rudy was a keg of dynamite ready to go off. Thank the Lord for intervening and bestowing the light of day! Only a cigarette paper away from doing the unthinkable, that was Rudy. As it goes now, harming her is not an option. He couldn't and wouldn't! His children, the rationale along with why should he do time or the chair for doing in a snake such as her. Although his feelings have mellowed even though brazen her ways, he despises Ellen greatly and always will.

Chapter 5

ALWAYS SHORT!

Throughout their married life seemingly they were always short on money. It making not the slightest difference how much revenue that had been generated, Rudy and Ellen were perpetually short of the capital seemingly necessary to surpass daily existence. Not once in awhile, but all the while, consistently. This overture showing additional mental vacancy on Rudy's part and correct you are. He should, did and does own up to this even though it is less than a positive virtue. The intention for reiterating the prior instance was to gain insight and reinforce your consciousness manifesting an understanding of Rudy's weakness and mental incompetence. Well, so you did not forget his inadequacies and that is reasonable!

Having no control of either/or, the mishap or the misfortune Rudy had married. The marriage, although unfortunate, a blessing of several precious children had been bestowed. At relation's end one had been lost in a heart- wrenching tragedy. The children mentioned had given him much pride and a feeling of need and a joy filled life. They are the breaths, the heart and beat of his being.

Getting sidetracked seems to be the way of the day. An attempt forthcoming, I will venture forward attempting not to go astray another time. The years trucking had been good to Rudy financially. Periodically, revenue quite sparse, consequently with Ellen's spending habits not advantageous to a desirable conclusion. The aftermath was an undesirable and final consequence, which in part, is beneficial to

Rudy. Indulging in habits so senseless, her, a matter of Rudy's observation. The perception resulting in the absolute reasoning for being continuously short of funds causing strain and getting a reprieve not in the realm of their futuristic agenda. Subsequently, a feeling of inadequacy in addition the birth of monumental despair. Poor Rudy!

At this point in time they managed to purchase a different house. Rudy went on to say this particular house was relatively nice. The man Rudy drove a truck for was leased to a prominent trucking company, subsequently when obtaining his own trucks he was able to lease to them also. The affluent uncle mentioned earlier gave Rudy money to get started. Another example of how Rudy's family immediate and not so immediate tried their hearts out to benefit the couple financially.

This is another example showing that Ellen was interested in her benefiting and only her. She never made an attempt to pay back the money acquired from Rudy's relatives. It doesn't say anything for Rudy to have let this type of behavior go unchecked. On his behalf pointing out it needs to be, taking care of his business left his hands full. Ellen handled all the money all the time. When bringing mention of pay back of borrowed money she would go off on Rudy pointing out how selfish his relatives were. Putting him down making fun of his disabilities. He was a spineless broken man not realizing till this point in time that mental and physical attributes should not be taken for granted. He professes GOD should be thanked daily for the gifts that a person is blessed with at birth. These gifts he speaks of consist of coordination, mental health and including any other blessing of supremacy when born. Well, maybe not everything else such as a deceitful mind and overactive sexual needs but they wouldn't be a supreme blessing, supposedly. The czar of hell intervenes once in awhile! Rudy quick to point out on the Lord's behalf the devil interceded on her journey to day present. The prior statement is not a blessing anyway. Rather than blessing, perversion would suffice as description.

Ellen has to live with the derivative born from her self-gratifying ways, Rudy doesn't. Take it to the bank, she is miserable internally to the degree of crumbling. Knowing that portion of her more so than anyone, Rudy hypothesizes there is not any doubt about it she's crying and dying within. Right or wrong, Rudy hasn't a sympathetic bone in his body. What goes around comes around and Ellen's is emerging slowly but surely.

Chapter 6

DISCOMBOBULATING

A narrative: Rudy's son, Chris, returning home from college. The extreme excitement, the jubilance imposed from the greeting of Chris's younger sister. The baby sister and Chris's only sister whom he completely cherished. An I've missed you, love you, hello hug, commonplace, then the card. A card, the one she had found while attempting to locate one thing or another in her mother's nightstand. This particular card with cartoon characters depicting Mother and mother's boyfriend kissing on the front. The depiction an amoral action however mild when compared to the verbalism from within. Her boyfriend professing his love for her - noxious - in association with an immoral fixation, that was making love to her. Lastly, the obscure kiss in front of the mall, sending him to heaven. So romantic to remember grade school emotions. WOOO-WEEE!

Chris's Call

The call corroborating suspicions, then later devastation, a destructive conclusion and jeopardy, seeming without end. Rudy's reaction was that of "Oh, my GOD!" An unthinking reply and simultaneously shouting, "What's the matter?" Rudy unaware it was to be a nightmare for sure in his mind of shambles. A mind, his, reeling, later an inception nearly too unbearable for Rudy to recall. He was admirable, his determination, having a dire need of recounting his story, so nobly he attempted to fulfill the necessity having undeniable success. Involved were two calls, the first horrific relaying betrayal and then the second inferring destruction including an outcome simply devastating, here-forevermore. Saying his heart was shattered would be an understatement and Rudy trying to portray a calm even though insurmountable grief was whittling away his self-esteem. This to Rudy was and is overwhelming so consequently devastation is the controlling transgressor but having inexplicable courage and need he went on to recount a parable of heart-wrenching grief!

Rudy implied his son, having a personality of assurance and control, was frantic, in mental anguish choking with sobbing controls nonexistent. Reiterating once again, Rudy pointedly mouthed his son was frantic. The reason for such an out-of-character reaction came while making a noble attempt of trying to explain his mother is or was having an affair. Rudy came to the realization his son's dilemma was real, so consequently Rudy immediately attempted to calm his outraged son it being much out of character him acting in this nature. He was successful, unfortunately, a success that was to be short lived.

Rudy's awareness lacking and the kiss, the thought, unmerciful! What mall? To where and what was the paramour referring? There was no mall in their community. Wondering of possibilities, the interrogative, then his children's answer divulging information boggling the mind and this is when that ton of bricks dropped on Rudy. How remiss he had been and wonders how could this have happened to him? A question, that question which is predominantly the controlling function of post thoughts of the mind. Rudy's mind nearly ruined transcended the horror of a frivolous adventure. Then at that time he attempted to render an understanding of the dismay encircling his caricature.

Can You Believe?

One fall weekend, the excuse, school shopping, Ellen took herself and Rudy's princess to the metropolis. While there they contacted Ellen's lover boy. At this juncture, this slimeball joined them for breakfast. Concluding breakfast, then proceeding to the motel room of their occupancy. Why? Rudy questioned and had no earthly idea of what would to be sufficient as an answer? At that time, Rudy's princess sought permission to retrieve something of importance to her from the car. Upon receiving consent, she left promptly then returned with the same promptness. The punctual return surprising her mother and boyfriend, hence upon entry caught them kissing. The moral of an amoral parable, the princess brighter than the two imbeciles she was dealing with played dumb. A pretense of noticing not a thing, therefore the happenstance entry was not an issue. Fooling Mother so consequently discovery not in the realm of bother! Do you suppose her brain continues to reside in the South? Duh!

The entirety of the stay, Rudy knew nothing of and can venture only to surmise the kiss no doubt having taken place at one of the many malls in the area. With that observation portrayed consciously in a vivid manner, I will revert to the call.

According to Rudy, valor best describes his son's attempt to read the card. Emotions and control of these emotions were nonexistent. Rudy expressed, recounting and saying that it was needless to point out that Chris' speech for the most part was incomprehensible. Rudy went on to say that his, Rudy's, undivided attention along with much effort subsequently was able to conceive the content of this card. Believe you me, the out-of-control response is understandable. War and being old enough fight in one, but still a child in reality concerning his parents. You know, a child's mommy, his daddy, then realizing a parent who represented morality but only in a noncommittal nth degree was amoral and superficial. Completely ruinous of a child's mental well- being.

Unfortunately, or probably more correct to say fortunately, even in Ellen's moments of extra marital bliss, she did and does love him, Rudy added as an afterthought. This may be odd, but he was very adamant about his standpoint on this conjecture that included the concerns of mental hardships posed on oneself. Rudy seemed to have been predisposed concerning Ellen's ability to withstand these afflictions and communicated to me that the end result would be her suffering forever more! Good, was his uncompromising remark of excessive satisfaction?

Rudy's assurance, including a sober persona and an aura of it, will work out settled him immensely. They visited for a short, both expressing their love for each other, then saying their farewells in their own way, Rudy saying "See ya," his son saying "Later," his famed goodbye.

The next days seemed a lifetime in length changing Rudy's life at this time for all time. At the interval in topic, Rudy hadn't decided if the change was for the good, bad or indifferent. Ideas were askew but surely, he felt it would be for the good. For the life in him he is unable to see how it could be anything but good. Time will tell.

Will It Ever End?

Praying for omission of an echoing plea, yet every day the voice, humiliated, a heartbroken son and wondering, is omission an option? This was and is Rudy's turbulent thoughts of question. This something he has prayed for but not overly sure it will come to pass. His son's voice bloodcurdling, crying, choking, sobbing. This out-of-control cluster of emotions, the most heart-wrenching sound to have experienced in his lifetime. Your assumption I am sure is completely correct. Rudy still hears Chris pleading, an anxious young man wanting and looking for an answer where in all reality there was and is no answer.

The inaugural step of many to follow was very difficult. The difficulty, massive, was the first step and implementing that first directed step towards the end! Never, ever again to be blinded by loyalty and love was an assertion Rudy made quite candidly.

His mind a maze and understandably so when taking into consideration the foray of mind-boggling events leading to this array of mental fatality. Thinking of probabilities and possibilities next to come, astounded to say the least and another step taken towards the **end of a beginning**. What was there to do? A question lacking an answer. Considering and groping for the illusive explanation, Rudy continued to the truck stop of choice. Wishing he had cigarette! His intent was indulging in a nasty habit he had given up years before, therefore a major malfunction was trying to transcend. What was he thinking? Hell, he hadn't smoked a cigarette for a lot of years, the desire was uncalled for but he was wishing for a Camel regardless. He had the first drag gloriously entrenched in his mind recalling the taste and the gratification that would encompass that first sniff of smoke then the inhale. He had Camels stuck on his mind, he thought, *Heck, Camels is the only brand that ever was worth a darn; I've got to stick to my guns.* Rudy had said or people who knew him wouldn't give his statements of one thing or another a second thought. This I suppose to seem a little odd but a valid assessment so I concur wholeheartedly.

Rudy informed himself that he was self-destructing but of course this self- imposed accusation did not help the ungovernable urge facing him, control nonexistent. Getting an argument from within of an accusation of mental infirmity Rudy did not. Arriving at the truck stop, he immediately parked his large car. At this time, he stepped out and sauntered to the inside, at which time he purchased a pack of Camels. Having paid for them, immediately ripped open the package and without hesitation promptly placed one in his mouth. He then lit it and the savory smell of the smoke had such an aroma, wonderful, more marvelous than he had anticipated then the foreseen inhale. He knew better, nevertheless instead of drawing the coveted smoke into his lungs gently so as not to choke he had the feeling of invincibility, including an attitude of I've been here, done that before so he sucked in hard and deep. This action of insanity resulted in an episode of suffocation nearly choking him to death. He well-nigh blacked out. Man, them things were stout; yea, but not as stout as Rudy seemed to think he was. So he pretended? Looking back, a query, wondering how in the hell he ever smoked those nasty things? Only about a cigarette paper away from choking to death and too damn dumb or rather proud, proud of what eludes him, to admit it to anyone, even to himself that he had made a mistake! ☺ :

Chapter 7

THE MIND

G rief, something everyone experiences at one time or another, is a rather complex emotion. These emotions instill curiosity and that being emotions are necessary. The emotions I speak of have to do with love, death, birth, jealousy, murder, sadness and just about anything good, bad or evil. Say some emotions that promote feelings of hate or discontent are not needed we could do with or without. On the contrary, let me explain. I expect readers to be astonished with a scenario like I just suggested and understandable so! Chances are my perception may be wrong, so allow me to explain my theory of affirmation. I perceive, without grief you haven't a way to appreciate the joy of goodness or blessings. Returning to grief, an emotion that sometimes causes insurmountable mountains to climb, is a complexity too entailed to understand, no doubt necessary. Remember this thought as you continue to read of Rudy. Certain emotions can cause a sane man to act insane and an insane man to become rational and getting even, even if even is light-years away.

At this juncture, Rudy heading for the house was the choice of choices so he boarded his big truck (he preferred to refer to his truck as his large car) then spinning her around on a dime leaving nine cents change and setting sail. The super slab nonending with common sense absent, he proceeded home at a high rate of fuel consumption. Personal safety not a concern, consequently allowing all five hundred horses to have their head without governable intervention! Go, cowboy, and he lives to talk the tale!

Guesstimating at approximately one hundred fifty miles into his journey, Rudy stopped at a truck stop he patronized from time to time and promptly proceeded to a casino. Uncharacteristic of Rudy, he played a couple of slots, then noticing a reflection in a mirror and wondered who that poor rascal was. A double take and then recognizing it to be himself who was staring back. Then immediately thinking, *you poor son-of-a-bitch*. Rationalization of the thought, everyone needs sympathy from time to time he supposed. What a sorry looking, pathetic individual he must have been. Leaving before anyone recognized him was the choice of the moment, least ways that was his intentions. Now or then he couldn't say if he was successful but at any rate his intentions were as implied.

When leaving this establishment, he risked a question to himself as to why he stopped there. Hell, why did anyone stop there was the query of himself? The only women who stopped at places like that were not ladies but those who were looking to borrow a joystick from some unsuspecting Jake! Sort of like the soon, and I might add not soon enough to be, ex-wife Rudy suggested!

Departing from the casino, Rudy advanced to his ride, unlocked the door at which time he stepped in, sat, buckled, fired her up, warmed a bit, slipped her into gear and proceeded homeward bound. At about four or five hours, give or take a minute or two, into his trip, sleep became an issue. Not wanting to become a statistic, Rudy pulled into a parking area intending to nap. Strange it seems, rather odd he supposes but attempting to sleep was to no avail. Only when driving sleep was attainable. He infers this to be rather asinine. Considering maybe, maybe not?

Perturbed, understandably so, so not being able to sleep and at the same time him being so immensely tired. His next option was to like it, to lump it, or saddle and ride. His choice was the latter.

Stepping outside and stretching came next. "Boy, that felt good," he said. Then continuing to do a walk around inspection, bumping tires, checking lights for correct operation so on and so forth. Completing without delays a process that had become second nature from repetition he then boarded, released the air, put her in gear and eased on to the super slab with completion of this journey on his mind.

Approximately another four hours of land air travel, the first portion of Rudy's journey was completed. Arriving at his attorney's office, then in addition informed him of the dilemma facing he himself, Rudy, and relaying his intentions of divorce, which would necessitate his assistance entailing filing for a divorce. Then the question, a question that was completely ludicrous in Rudy's opinion, which was, and Rudy quoted, "Are you sure? Understand it is my moral obligation and ethics of law to ask you that question." "In my opinion, that was as ridiculous a statement as the question," Rudy stated. Then he asked the question that answered itself. "Tell me when a lawyer truly ever worried about ethics or morality, unless it was to keep his own butt out of a sling? That's right, not never, not ever! Doubt it and be wrong." Given that question, it takes minimal thought and an answer of never is a no- brainer and no doubt correct. ☺☹

Next came a reply from within a broken and confused, yet stately torso, Rudy saying, "I'm not sure. You know, the kids, how will they handle it? I am not one-hundred percent sure because of them." He promptly told Rudy that it could wait. Saying it didn't have to be done at that moment. Well, what proceeded next was the most monumental bunch of stupidity that ever came from within him, Rudy implied. That stupidity went something like this and Rudy said, "Guess I'll wait. I'll see what my feelings are after a few days. Well, I shouldn't have done that because it turned out to be more than a year and a few thousand dollars." Goes to show you that attorneys are not so brilliant after all. They have a license to legally steal, plain and simple. (*Not all attorneys will fall into this category but most do Rudy suggested.*)

Rudy gathered himself, put the divorce papers in his briefcase just in case he would decide to proceed with his original motive. Dispensing of a proper thank-you and good-bye, then removing himself from the office of law and commenced homeward. Traveling at such a tremendously high rate of speed, Rudy is probably fortunate to still be among the living.

"The evening was rather pleasant for that time of year," Rudy suggested, "and one way of looking at it I figure is that Mother Nature was with me, for how long I did not know." He implied,

"Understand the part of the country that I am talking of, the weather can change in a heartbeat." To continue, while journeying that evening Rudy had a very tough ride being quite difficult and containing himself didn't seem to be in the noncommittal plan for a quiet drive home that night. Consequently, he attempted to contact Paul, the Shadow, by telephone. To elaborate on him a piece of work, that one, which should have been flushed at birth. He was and is the biggest, fattest, amoral piece of monkey dung that ever crawled from within a sewer since time began. The phone call was a little on the moronic side of intelligent, but in defense of Rudy, his mind was having problems staying coherent, which would have been conducive to the degree of irrational problems staring him in the face.

Well, Ellen, shopping she had gone with her father and mother. Pointless in mention, telephone conception with him was not possible. So next best, Rudy simply left a charming message asking if their offspring of amoral activities, Ellen, had mentioned if her boyfriend's piece of pride was larger than his own modesty. "You know," Rudy said, "they never replied." This is an explicit example of the inconsiderate feces they are. ☺ This example exhibits consideration and was not in the realm. They never did let him know! So, he tried a second option, inquiring of Ellen the posed question. She said, "No." Rudy wondered if she lied. Rudy implied a habitual liar such as her in all likelihood probably did. "You know, once a liar always a liar," Rudy stated setting, staring in a state of bewilderment and wondering why, what had he done to deserve such a voracious verdict without an indictment to supersede his treatment.

Traveling the night away, fretful, not understanding the finality entangling his own, Rudy's consciousness, perceiving realization would be a long time to come. Feeling let down and betrayed, he was able to see not a thing is permanent and nothing should be taken for granted. Included in this mirage of collective nothings would-be marriage, freedom and life in general, as you will see later.

Chapter 8

THE ARRIVAL

Arriving in town and a feeling of dread was sweeping over Rudy. "The morning was oh so beautiful. The time a mite early so consequently Ellen had not prematurely arrived to work," Rudy pointed out. Then he went on to say he needed to bring to attention how difficult it was to speak of the ex without using superlatives like whore, bitch and slut, to name only a few lexicons that would suffice for her description. Senseless to mention why, but Rudy attempted to nap while waiting for the pretender to arrive at work. "In all reality, it was a shame napping when the morning was so beautiful," he said. "A winter morning and looking at myself I was disgusted, because me, Rudy, who loves nature so and was in the process of letting it slide by, a morning without notice and appreciating a gift from God. There would be many mornings similar to that particular morning so luxurious and pleasant, but in all reality," he interjected, "I may not be around to enjoy them." He said, "I hope you understand that apathy or being oblivious to a natural phenomenon such as that is inexcusable, to say the least." This stunned me and as I set peering my heart couldn't help but hurt for him. Rudy appeared to be broken and beat, having little alternative. I must go on and say that appearance is exactly what it was and is. It was what it implied — appearance — because for Rudy the fight had only just begun.

Ellen arrived at length. Rudy's heart racing and pounding the anticipation of an inevitable confrontation at a peak. It was only a fragment of an unyielding episode nearing a time and place. This instance at that time, he speculated, wondering if Ellen was even a little remorseful and decided to put that thought of delirium out of his mind, knowing it was only hopeful or maybe better said uplifting ideas with intent, subconsciously to massage a bruised ego. "That makes sense, doesn't it?" Rudy questioned.

Rudy, wearing his cap backward and until that day never had he worn it in that fashion, looking like he'd come out of a horror movie, dirty, needing sleep, walking up to the door. Reaching for the handle, hesitated then gave a pull. Finding it locked, he was not at all surprised. Simply standing staring at the inside, the door being glass. Ellen came to the door at which time they proceeded to her car and went for a drive. Immediately she thanked Rudy for not blowing a gasket and causing a scene. "You know," he said, "that was the first and only time in their years of togetherness that she ever thanked him for anything," and he said he definitely did mean anything. Then the lies that came were in abundance. Reflecting, he doesn't believe the self- serving bitch told him one breath of truth. "No matter," he said, "I wasn't surprised in the least." She had the audacity to blame Rudy for her going down on and for a short little piece of homely whatever you would prefer to call him.

"If she, being the Pretender, took off her makeup you would understand very quickly how pretentious she was and still is." Rudy explains, "For sure without her makeup, she is one ugly woman." Adding, "The nearest thing describing her would be the resemblance of a plucked chicken's ass." So in regards to that affirmation, Rudy ventured to imagine if Mr. Boyfriend saw her in that state, his kickstand would shrivel and drop off. "No doubt about it!" he assured. ☺

Satisfaction of explanations not in-vision. At that time, he decided to proceed back to his place of origination so put his ride in the wind. Rudy could and would get under another load going to the coast. After journeying back to his origination, he managed to secure a load at which time he loaded and headed journey bound. In a matter of about fifteen hours he managed to roll by the place he at that time still called home. Arrived and promptly parked his truck and proceeded to the ex's place of employment. At which time he confronted her with the proposition of her taking off work a couple hours early, they then would go home and get reacquainted. Abruptly telling him that she had an overabundance of work to do, needing her immediate attention. *(Remember that excuse and later decide if she was telling the truth or just another lie, also remarking that she and Rudy needed to get respect for each other. Hello! Where did she assume that Rudy would fit into a scenario to that effect)?*

At this instance, Rudy loaded in his truck and proceeded on his journey. Getting approximately one hundred fifty miles into his travel plan, stopping, Rudy called home. His son answered, they visited for a period then Rudy asked to talk to Mom. Chris at that time informed his dad that his mother was at some mythical party. At which time Chris reminded his father that her lover boy was to be back in town. This instance of brains out to lunch shows how mentally depleted Rudy was. He knew he was to be back in town and had entirely dismissed this knowledge, so consequently he had departed. Needless to say, a supposition of what was taking place in his absence was mind crippling. He, to this day, cannot understand where the strength was derived to deliver and pick up.

Determination

His inbound load was one of the most mind- challenging difficult loads he has ever handled to this day, along with the undue stress Ellen had unleashed on him, was overwhelming to say the least.

During the interim between delivery and pick up only being a frog's hair away from going completely bonkers, Rudy contacted Ellen's folks. Apologizing to them for actions beyond his control. Crazy! Which was an explicit example of the off wall mental incapability he was dealing with. The concept of apologizing should have never entered his thoughts. Yet, still trying to be or do what was wanted of him, as inexplicable as it may be, hunting for an apocalypse unconsciously, wanting the insanity to end. Crying, sobbing like a baby, begging, gasping, choking, pleading for forgiveness. What's this? Yea, that's right, overboard with grief … and humiliation. Incomprehensible, to any and all, unless you have walked the walk.

Trying to keep control of his mind, attempting to get home for Christmas was going to be a chore. A time of joy for all! That not to be the case in this instance. Meaning, how was he to enjoy a time of year like Christmas when a pretentious, evil, harlot had put him into an out-of-control situation completely mentally incapacitating him! A woman Rudy had trusted beyond a reasonable doubt who acted like the epitome of morality and again having unadulterated undeserved trust yet exposing herself as the exact opposite. Will wonders ever cease?

The Inbound Load

With much work physically and approximately fourteen hours of steady labor they, they, being his laborers, he had hired, and Rudy himself making a total of four men managed to load his trailer. Then came the extraordinary journey home for Christmas. A time and place he would forget if possible, still not having peace of mind that Ellen was behaving.

Circumstances inundating Rudy, merciless as snow in a March storm being what they were. Understanding the mental duress that had transpired of which Rudy was pinned beneath should not be difficult. The journey home, a ride of torture to say the least. Weary and once again able to sleep only while driving and for that reason he wasn't able to maintain a conciseness present enough to operate his large car. It was a devoted effort arriving home without becoming a statistic of fatality on the holiday highways.

Rudy's son called informing him his mother was with her parents in her absence of the night and early morning disappearance. The dates of the disappearance being the evening of and the morning after Rudy had departed. This bit of news sedated him, only momentarily. It just didn't ring true he didn't question only quietly surmised the coincidence of this and it being accurate, it being the period of time her partner of sexual intimacy was in town. Nevertheless, it settled him down a bit, although short lived.

Anyway, as the story goes, arriving home for Christmas, he tried to have a decent time but was mentally inept so wasn't able to enjoy the holiday like he normally would have, him having children. These children were his pride and joy. He is sorry beyond comprehension not being able to shake the feeling of despair and disgust that had encompassed his existence. He was home for Christmas Eve. Christmas Day and to this day he can only remember one thing he received for Christmas. Sad, allowing events of the day to dominate actions skewing the memory of such a glorious time of year. Descriptions and memories of that particular Christmas is and will be a memory of complete chaos and sorrow!

How it came to be and then went, Rudy may not ever understand or realize. What Rudy was speaking of was Christmas.

You know the time, everyone, one and all, are supposed to put aside differences and celebrate a holiday of giving and receiving. I might add to the special day, the reason for such a day, that being the birth of Jesus Christ, our Lord and Savior. A detail not so minor and having a major implied meaning if acknowledged in the slightest!

Chapter 9

WONDERS

According to Rudy, it was a major ordeal. That is, him getting back on track the day after Christmas. Slowly together with much effort it was a feat in itself boarding his truck. With this accomplished, he soon afterward headed to his proposed destination, with delivery on the mind. The delivery went well when lo and behold he managed to obtain a shipment, its destination right back to the customer he had previously serviced. Unusually and commonly, this did not happen, a coincidence but much appreciated so as to promote a feeling of ease. This was a feel-good feeling that was seeping into Rudy's mindset. It was an infiltration of the mind that was a welcomed enticement, Rudy had explained because he wouldn't be wondering if finding his place of delivery would give him problems. He knew exactly where it was and how he would get there.

Now for those of you who do not know the expectations of a truck driver, or maybe better how the trucking industry functions, this was a major relief alleviating one problem so as to have one problem less to be dealt with.

Rudy managed to arrive home a couple days before New Year's and with much work was able to have relatively an enjoyable time. Taxing his mind and trying to find something special to do for New Year's Eve for his princess, a friend of his princess and finally least and last, Ellen, they ventured to another town for New Year's Eve. They stayed at motel and you guessed it, according to Rudy, Ellen was a fourteen-Carrot idiot. Short on money with Ellen long on selfish wants created a problem. Finding a ring she desired and caused a scene. Hell, the cost was only a hundred-dollar bill plus a little change for the governor. Actually, he was a tad short on green backs so considering their current problems Rudy didn't feel compelled to stretch his dollars. Well, right away, Mrs. Manic Depressant[11] started to give him grief. Immediately, Rudy became panic stricken, wanting an attempt of complacency as to show his princess that everything was going to be okay! That's when, you guessed it, attempting to develop a tranquil environment for Rudy's princess, his truly, that being Rudy, gave in to the Ellen's whims and bought her that ring. That's correct, like a spineless worm, Rudy purchased it for her. □ Is spineless correct or does concern for his daughter's metal stability describe more precisely his plan?

It seemed being content possibly was only for his dreams and leaving their problems at rest was only in the realm of distant possibilities not probabilities. Love, hope and approval have astronomical influences on common sense. Therefore, discretion, predominately the paramount portion of the aforesaid God-given talent, was absent. No, not just a little misdirected, not in the picture. Null and void! Get it? Rudy was very secure with his mindset. He stated if whomever didn't get it, he'd say a prayer for whoever and at the same time ask the Lord if He the Lord would instill into Rudy's understanding why someone would be is so brain-dead and dumb. Rudy had stated that he did not mean to be cruel but there would be no other explanation for whoever believes differently. Quite adamant on this subject he spoke of people's inability to discern in order to ascertain the full magnitude of topic in question. He went on to say he would say a prayer for anyone or everyone that stupid, whomever they might be.

The onset gets better in a worse way, the irrational logic of one Ill-logical, self-destructing piece of work such as Rudy's wife, Ellen. Rudy's intent, trying to salvage the evening for everyone involved, subsequently he did purchase her the ring. Their anniversary was nearing and implying he never bought her anything for the special occasion before so she guessed what's the difference. This particular statement held a noncommittal aura asserting that Rudy had better buy that for her or else. Well, push came to shove, so inherently Rudy knew the choice had been made for him. He bought it for her and as so many other times in his pathetic married life he simply

---

[11]   *MANIC DEPRESSANT: Overactive aggressive sexual conduct.*

wishes he would have found out what the, or else, would have been.

In the evening they went to a quality restaurant for dinner with immense expectations, this was Rudy's planned extravaganza. He added regardless of disallowance of an accommodating other half it was enjoyable, the meal and two-thirds of his company was anyway. His princess and her friend seemed to have a pleasant time, for which he was quite thankful. That was a positive.

His memory fails him, but concluding the evening meal Rudy conveyed it seems as though they partook of a show at the cinema, then proceeded afterwards to their motel at which time they retired and entertained themselves briefly viewing television. Content of objectivity while engaging in a little television is eluding but seems observing an old movie or something to that effect was the case.

It actually makes no difference what they did, for other than for the girls, it was a complete failure. Wondering at this particular time what in the devil Rudy had done to deserve the punishment he had been exposed to while being married to a self-absorbed nymphomaniac such as Ellen. At that time, he couldn't answer the question and still he is held at bay for he thinks it may more than likely be a question that cannot possibly be answered. One thing for sure, Rudy presumes, in a realistic affirmation, it never will be! Only hypothetically can this ploy have a resolution of finality!

Eventually sleep slithered in and one by one slumber was brought into existence. This initiated until total concession of consciousness was the occurrence. Rudy, being rather beat with that in mind, he was not one of the casualties of fatigue so was unable to acquire a restful night of sleep. On that account, when morning came it was difficult for him to rise and shine even though he was already awake when their wakeup call pierced the silence of the morning.

Still acting like a gentleman that he inherently was, Rudy allowed Ellen to shower first and put on her face. He went on to say, that in itself was monumental achievement. How she could sculpture a face such as she put on in such a short aggregate of time was beyond Rudy. Actually, it wasn't so fast but meticulous work such as he spoke of Michael Angelo taking years to accomplish, not just a couple of hours.

After treating themselves to a rather scrumptious breakfast they went shopping with the objective to purchase a gift for Rudy's princess, her birthday was approaching. Rudy's birthday was prior to hers but that's okay, his princess was first in thought and will remain with that domain as her birthright. Debate not an option in regards to that issue. He is sure everyone will understand why and has a closed mind when his princess is the realm of consideration. "In the case there is defiance relating to this topic and you don't get it you have my unadulterated condolences for being absolutely so stupid," Rudy stated, "and needless to say, you are beyond help of any degree, shape or form." He also made plain his feelings saying it is too bad that stupidity in that degree is not deadly, or such a painful ordeal it would be the only thing to entertain the clouded mind, from now till death do you part.

Arriving home that afternoon they took Rudy's princess's friend home. She too was a princess just not to the degree as Rudy's princess was and continues to be. Rudy sounds a little one-sided but that can be understood. They thanked her for accompanying them to the city and would she please tell her dad and mom hello for them.

They headed for the house and Mrs. Nymph started her usual accusations of how self-centered Rudy was. How he only thought of himself with no concern for anyone else. They watched football on the tube[12] for period of time. That evening they were, or at least Rudy was, rather exhausted so retired earlier than usual.

The day following, Rudy proceeded to retire the Christmas lights for another year. Not a small feat to say the least. His son, Chris, helped him, accomplishing this necessary bit of work in a short accumulate of time. His son helped immensely, what a young man with such a promising future. He had it going on, as the young people would say about someone who is succeeding with aspirations such as his. Rudy simply says he R-O-C-K- E-D. He and Rudy were tight, similar to the rind on a watermelon. A fortunate blessing to have. You know a connection as such. A father and son, but more than that, they were FRIENDS. BEST FRIENDS!

---

[12]   *TUBE: Slang for television*

Chapter 10

DOES IT MATTER?

Earlier, Rudy failed to mention that Ellen and he visited a psychologist in a nearby town. The psychologist of topic inquired a number of point-blank questions, and to Rudy's dismay, she lied like a rug. Completely, absolutely and deliberately giving answers of misdirection or untruths. So actually making not the tiniest of differences of knowledge Rudy knew to be true. He had to like it or lump it. He didn't like it so the next option was taken.

Mentioning the psychologist is important. Rudy's son, a couple days after New Year's, transported him for another appointment to visit this professional. Rudy finished his visit, then at that time, his son and he proceeded to a sandwich house. They kicked back, ordered a couple of drinks and decided to hang for awhile. At this time, Chris had the urge to present an untold truth concerning an occasion that been in question earlier in the transpiration of key information. A truth such as to where his mother was that mysterious evening, morning of her disappearance. The truth was as suspected Chris divulged his mother was with her lover boy. Then the deplorable act of intimidating Chris by requesting him to call Rudy and giving forth a statement of misdirection. The information he relayed to his dad was Mom had been with her parents. The filthy lowlife mind-manipulating harlot told Rudy's son if he was to tell him the truth and his dad wrecked it, it would be his fault. With pressure to that degree, putting the screws to him in such a lowlife manner, Chris believed her and felt he hadn't a choice. The pressure of this innuendo was an insurmountable burden to bear. Chris's lie to Rudy was forgiven immediately. He was so careworn over lying to Rudy, containing himself nearly impossible and he cried. He was most afraid Rudy would be angry and consequently was distraught beyond description. At that interim, Dad told Son not to worry about it at which time he threw his arms around Rudy and told him he loved him and gave his dad one of his famous hugs. That was the part of the pie Rudy really enjoyed. The center, if you follow his thought process. Their son actually was Rudy's son beyond any reasonable doubt regardless of genes, recessive or otherwise. Rudy's and only Rudy's!

Rudy guessed to be plagued with this next tribute would be a wonderful thing. His son absolutely did not hate anyone. Luckily for his mother, Rudy assured with an attitude such as that if his son did, his mother would have an inside track of being first on the list, then number two would be Paul, the shadow. That's a certainty beyond any discredit. As he sat there relaying his narrative and fighting tears of distress having great difficulty speaking in a coherent, audible perception. The difficulty for Rudy was withstanding the emergence of tears that inadvertently surfaced while witnessing his son's excruciating pain. I also was tearful making it a feat writing.

Rudy can still hear, feel and see his son's fright in worry his dad would be outraged since he had lied to him. The wonderful thing is Rudy also can still see the relief in his son' face when he let Chris know he knew it was something out of his control and he could not help it. Informing his son that his dad still loved him as much and probably more than Chris loved him because as Rudy told him, he was older and knew how to love better. Chris looked at him laughed and said, "I'm sure." That, I'm sure held the connotation of — Only in your dreams, Old Man!

Chapter 11

MIXED FEELINGS

The difficulty evoked sharing the recall of this information was immense but he continued at length. A few afternoons following New Year's, his son approached Rudy requesting permission to venture to the country. His intention? Visiting his girlfriend. "Sure, I'm not leaving until late tomorrow! You haven't left yet?" Rudy replied smiling. "Cool," Chris responded as he gave his dad a big old hug then reinforced his feelings once again by saying, "I love you. Later!" What a lucky man Rudy was having a son such as that! A type of loyalty and love worth his weight in gold, his son, many times over! The day odd, a feeling of quietness and there was no reason that Rudy could put a finger on but it seemed strange, seemingly different. Rudy would later realize why.

Wondering the upshot of his future, Rudy floated around the house. He attempted to do a few things, exactly what he fails to remember explicitly. One thing for sure, whatever it was it was probably frivolous in nature and such a description probably best describes the inconsequential agenda he had laid for himself that day.

Then Here Came Ellen

Then arriving home shortly after departure from her place of employment was Ellen. Rudy's princess was home necessitating a return to school after the upcoming weekend. Her mother making her appearance was in need of an attitude adjustment and it would have been banner but no such luck. Still acting like an imbecile, not uncommon for an egocentric agenda such as hers truly.

It seems as though he had ordered a pizza Rudy suggested and ventured to and from bringing it home for all to feast. He attempted to watch TV periodically and mysteriously could not shake the unsettled feeling with which he was encompassed. He wondered what the problem was and reasoned it to be due to the extraordinary stress that chastised his mental stability. This was his logic and not being able to put a finger on it for sure decided to retire.

Not long after allowing the comfort of his king-size water bed to caress and cuddle his fatigued body the mistaken half of his marriage made her appearance and commenced to disengage her facial sculpture of the early morning. It, a substantial feat removing her Pulitzer Prize winning sculpture, a work of detail, from her face, a face of abysmal unsightliness. By the time she accomplished this art of destruction, Rudy was getting a little put out. In appearance she seemed to be taking her time. Rudy assumed her objective was cracking his composure, but he shared he was proud his poise sufficed. Painstaking her effort of massive destruction and having finality resulting with her also coming to bed.

At this crossroad, Rudy decided to broach the subject of the sexual interlude with her friend of intimate relations. How she chose not to discuss the intervening period is beyond Rudy. In all reality, Rudy felt a need for her to project reasoning for such an out-of-place occurrence but she didn't and did not. It wasn't of importance to her so not in the realm of undertaking. She simply expected Rudy to accept the truism that she had balled[13] another man, no questions asked, just accept it. Not being ready to accept such a request of precedence Rudy rose, stating with certainty, that he was out of there. Next came the donning of his attire along with the completion of brewing a thermos of coffee. Standing in the kitchen door, his princess begging him not to leave. Then Rudy told her he was sorry, but guessed he had better leave. Telling her good-bye stepping out of the door while his princess was crying, begging her mommy not to let him go, pulling at her housecoat and pleading with her, "Please, Ma-Ma, pleeease, don't, Ma-Ma, don't let him go." At that time, her mother turned and pushed her back and angrily and snapped at her saying, "Don't!" She declared there was nothing she could do if her father wanted to leave. So hard, him relaying feelings as such with

____

[13]   *Balled: To have intercourse just for the heck of it.*

him dealing with this atrocity of overbearing emotions. The emotions I speak of were the problems that were haunting him at this displeasing time. Enforcing his love to Her Majesty, his princess, assuring her he would be okay and simultaneously telling her to smile 'cause he would see her soon. "Bye, love. Bye, bye!" Rudy said. Then closing the door and started his trek of several blocks to his truck. Arriving in due course, he called his son and conveyed his intentions of departure. He simply informed him that Mom and he were not yelling and screaming but the air was rather abrasive so Rudy decided to remove himself from the scenario. Expressing his feelings of dismay, he conveyed seeing Chris the next day wasn't at that time an option. Immediately, his son voiced not to concern himself with such a minuscule problem as that, assuring Dad he would see him in the not too distant future. Rudy told Chris he had to get fuel so he had better get going. His son inquired how long that it would take him. Rudy replied probably an hour or so by the time he got to the truck stop and put in a couple hundred gallons of fuel. At this time, Chris informed his dad he might come in and see him off but not to worry if he didn't make it. Rudy told him to drive carefully and not to go home and get in his mother's face. He agreed to be careful, not to worry; he was cool. Rudy gave him his love and Chris advised Rudy the same. Rudy said, "See ya." Again, his son said, "Later." Rudy thought at that time and wished he had just a fraction of his son's cool, but knowing all too well, it was not to be then or ever.

Rudy washed his windows extra proficient, being meticulous hoping his extra slow mobility may give his son extra time to arrive. It didn't happen and Rudy was slightly concerned, but he figured probably an insurmountable amount of kissy face was the culprit concerning his no show. Remembering how it was when he was young. Still moving rather slowly, hoping for his arrival which was not to be. Darn it anyway, was Rudy's thought! Rudy paid for his fuel and eased onto that never-ending stretch of asphalt. He put it into the wind,[14] hammer down.[15] He was tired but had plenty of time so about an hour or so later Rudy pulled into a truck stop and went to bed. He attempted to sleep, but like an elusive dream, sleep was evasive as well. Very early the ensuing morning, Rudy, sitting on the edge of his bed sleep had been eluding, so consequently clothed himself preparing to continue his journey. Mind overworked and agitated to say the least, then his phone rang. Rudy fumbled for his telephone, when locating it pushed the answer button. "Hello?" The voice on the other end was Ellen, "Is that you?" Then Rudy said, "Who in the hell else would it be? Did you mean to call Mr. Lover Boy?" "Stop it!" she snapped. "Chris wrecked his car coming in from the country!" "He was killed, wasn't he?" "Yes," was her reply. "Where are you?" was the next inquiry. "Down the road a piece," said Rudy. "I'll be home directly. Tell your dad to get his ass out of my house or I'm going to kick it out when I arrive." Moral of the story is she didn't and Rudy attempted to put knots on his head. Rudy hit the son- of-a-bitch when actually it would have been more prudent just to shoot him. His other son jumped him from the rear with the help of his grandma and mother along with the help of his grandpa after he got his senses back in place wrestled Rudy to the ground. When they got him down, the big fat S.O.B. was sitting in the middle of him and along with the help of the other three, thus Rudy was rather immobile. What happened next was Fats commenced telling Rudy how he had fought the biggest, toughest guys in the country and Rudy wasn't anything. His son choking him using his thumb in the soft of Rudy's throat, making it difficult to talk or breathe. When able to get his wind and speaking was possible Rudy asked, "Why is it if you're so tough did it take four of ya all to put me down? Tell me that, big boy." Then came the predisposed reply, "So I wouldn't have to hurt you." What a saint! Wasn't Rudy lucky? So affected, Paul's masquerade. What a pretentious puke he was and is, Rudy being immobile consequently wasn't able to contest him at that time? The fat S.O.B. weighing a mere two hundred forty-five pounds and perched in the middle of him and bragging what a tuff bastard he was and is. What a loser!

Mental Cruelty

At that time, Rudy broached the subject of a past episode regarding mental abuse. Rudy cited the subject matter regarding Paul's insinuation of the affluent uncle Rudy had mentioned earlier. To continue, Paul at one time implied to Rudy that this uncle of subject had inherited his wealth. The ulterior motive was screwing with

---

¹⁴ *Put it in the wind: Leave on your journey.*
¹⁵ *Hammer down: Driving at a high rate of speed.*

Rudy's head, he feels. With Rudy practically incapacitated and hardly capable of an existence, it is nesedless to point out that it was beyond his ability to act in defense of his uncle. Rudy reiterated that he, Rudy, was not quite at a hundred percent of mental capability, let alone his physical assets having gone south. A feeling of helplessness being inexplicable encompassed Rudy's character. Paul knew Rudy idolized his uncle so together with this innuendo would take unfair advantage of his mind, having at that time only a partial mind. Presupposing this does not substantiate Rudy's accusation; regardless, Rudy feels this was Paul's intention beyond any reasonable doubt. Seeing this is not a problem for Rudy and shouldn't be for anyone knowledgeable of Paul. This knowledge would include Paul's less-than-admirable character. Rudy recognized also that it made not a bit of difference what other people knew of Paul for they had not the stature needed to confront him so in turn making him take responsibility for his spiteful ways wasn't part of the picture.

Chapter 12

EXCUSES

Next, Paul's conundrum for financial embarrassment was Rudy. Implying, he understood Rudy's intentions were to come back to the family business and because of this belief the reason for his outlandish financial misstep in trying to expand. That was as Democrap as it gets, meaning like other demarcates Paul would not own up to his shortcomings. Rudy explained Paul was a professional at rebuking his misfortune. Seems a lowlife agenda and probably as lowlife as it gets considering Rudy's mental as well as physical challenges.

After the verbal altercation between them as he perched on top of Rudy, he asked, and Rudy quoted, "Got any witnesses?" Rudy asserted a reply of, "You know I don't. You're stupid but not ignorant enough to say that in front of anyone. You are a chicken shit and don't have the balls to say that in front of anyone." That coincides with him telling Rudy he should try to screw his mother-in-law. Remember? Mentioning that earlier too plays into making Rudy's point. Well, needless to say, Rudy damn sure didn't have any witnesses at that time either. "I should probably keep this remark to myself but feel it necessary to comment on his quest of amoral intent." Rudy concluded, "I wouldn't screw that rough-headed jezebel if she and I were both single and the only man and woman on earth so consequently I wasn't about to entertain the thought of doing such a hideous deed with my mother-in-law. Yuck!" ☹!

Meanwhile, before Rudy's questions, he was shaking like a dog passing barbed wire. Dripping blood on Rudy from the bruise and cuts Rudy managed to put on Paul's noggin. Telling his ugly other half, "Call the law, call the law, and hurry-up, call the law!" You know what? She did. Rudy settled down, not because he wanted to but because he thought it deemed necessary so he wouldn't have to go to jail. In his house, he told Paul to get out and you know the rest.

Some more on this perverted, sorry son-of-a-bitch and Satan. To sum up, Paul, a little more, he always bragged about how tough he was. His brag included how big, bad and ugly he was to his hired help. Big and ugly Rudy couldn't argue with so not having a difference he would concur on that point. Paul would also include how he did this and how he did that and was going to do a number of other things. He was in La-La land. Such a tough bastard, settling around the dinner table having for an audience of his wife, grandchildren, daughters, hired help or anyone who would listen and not challenge him or his statements of superiority. Often talking of the lackadaisical help. Included in his victims' ridicule was his neighbor's son who happened to be his relation of one way or another. Pieces of work pertaining to this type of riffraff never ceased to amaze Rudy. In an environment with others or where he may be tested, he was and is a sham, not having a backbone.

The one thing major that attributes to Rudy's nearly giving up is the betrayal of Rudy's number one son. Him blinded by a misplaced loyalty to his grandpa so learned quite well how to be a chicken shit and act like a tuff bastard when odds lay heavy in his favor, not being fair. Par for the course, don't you suppose?

His Son!

Rudy said he would like to elaborate on his son. At the time of childhood, he and Rudy were so very close. Rudy remembering upon his arrival at home, he in a relatively short period of time started driving truck. The excursions in his truck would keep him away from home for a day or two. When preparing to leave, his son would cry because he didn't want him to go. Rudy expressed his heart would cry with him. Once away and on the road, Rudy's baby blues would cry also. Not allowing himself to blubber in front of his precious little man. In these instances, Rudy would go out of his way to joke and attempt to be funny. Rudy added, "It worked some of the time, consequently once in a while I managed to get him to laugh." Very pleased with himself by that accomplishment. Rudy would feel very successful with himself when his son's feelings of despair were put aside, even if only momentarily!

In retrospect, Rudy realizes the terrible trauma that engulfed his precious little man. Out of his control, losing for a period of time his daddy, whom at that time he idolized. It was an ordeal the likes no one else can fathom. A betrayal not intentional on Rudy's part, but very real on his son's not understanding where his father went. Then Rudy returning home physically and leaving his mental and physical blessings elsewhere. Rough housing, a way of playing and naturally always letting him get the upper hand. He was Rudy's main man and talking of that Rudy came close to tears. His son's grandpa stepped in and did a lot for him and at the same time silently pulled him away from his dad. Financially not able to compete with the Paul, the Shadow, silently but surely bought and bribed his loyalty. Rudy agrees it was his fault to a degree. Rudy was too compliant to adversary implications. I suppose there is a possibility of this, although being a fact I would have to be very doubtful. I would have to question his assessment of this fable. He could not help his physical condition and mentally he was on vacation.

Then there was the Ellen. Money grubbing, spending cash like it grew on trees … literally. Self-centered and concerned with herself and only herself. Growing to adolescence then adulthood, having a self-centered father she learned well how to cheat, lie, steal and just plainly to be dropped off the old slim ball.

Chapter 13

INCOMPREHENSIBLE

Rudy wanted everyone to understand so pointed out that understanding disintegration of time was difficult! Rushing and not to be seized then disappearing. Comprehending time depravation difficult – time - being all there was and is? A deception! Akin to the scampering of hares. Yet dragging, comparable consistency to glacier movement. Inexplicable, but understandable? Rudy's world had come to an end, or so it seemed. In thought is it not understandable the abundance of disparity engulfing his insight, in essence he was in a state of chaos? Wondering, will normality return or will mass confusion be for evermore?

As with any and all things right, wrong or indifferent, this too would pass. Meanwhile, an interim of mental assassination many things evolving. Resulting in unrest and discontent. Rudy wishing, wanting and simply hoping for a reprieve from the insanity so normalcy could and would be compliant.

Time being a friend and foe simultaneously and moving with excruciating slowness. These particular instances vanishing, in your face was time then disappearing mysteriously, wondering where did it go, including speculation of how? Understanding was constantly eluding Rudy, yet he would strive to ascertain a comprehension all the while hoping his quest of grasping the fact would be rewarding and therefore he would be successful!

The Funeral

Chris's funeral was surreal, yet according to Rudy, the most gratifying funeral he'd ever been to. An overtone, suggesting a nightmare and included in this induction was an aura of mental instability. Undoubtedly correct, what she was and is. Pointing a finger - Rudy being the target - not realizing she had pointed three at herself. A pertinacious, self-patronizing, manic-depressant eluding admission of amoral activities. (*Theatrics at its best.*) While all the while carrying on a poor-me syndrome, nourished by the ever-growing disingenuous public scrutiny of Rudy. Mind manipulation, incidentally playing a significant role in public opinion.

The law ultimately is blind; life is not fair although no one claimed it was. Is this determination correct in a script environment, or do you believe in GOD? He says ask and you shall receive, but there is a catch to the asking and receiving: you must believe before you receive not after. There are stipulations on most everything, even from God. Ho hum! Life is not fair, which we determined earlier, so existence, quality existence depends on number one. Hence, opinions bully or no are in the hands of the subject of conversation. This sets a venue for actions on the behalf of Rudy. Nice times three what he'd have to be, or sharpen his survival instincts and simply defeat her at her own stratagem. Rudy wondered aloud if this would be possible?

A Call

One night, Rudy's telephone rang. He answered, "Hello" and had a pleasant surprise hearing his princess's voice from within. Rudy's "Hello," then "Hey, Daddy." "Well, helloooooo, princess, what is my honor to have such royalty call me at this time of night?" She giggled then, "When you coming home?" "Well, terd *[her brother's pet name]*, probably sometime tomorrow. Why do you ask?" "Don't come home! They're going to put you in jail." "Who's going to put me in jail?" "Mom called the county attorney; she accused you of following her the other night when you were at home. So, they're going to put you in jail. Mom said you broke the restraining order. That's why." "Bull shit!" Rudy spat. "I'd better hang up before Mom hears me talking. Love you, Daddy, be careful." "I will and thank you bunches for calling me, princess," Rudy replied. "You're welcome," came her reply. "Say, did I ever tell you who the prettiest girl in the whole wide world is?" Rudy asked. "Yyyeeesss," was her reply. "Well, did I ever tell you?" Cutting off Rudy with a "Yepper" was her quick response.

Doing this repetitively had developed into a game with them. Rudy asking the same questions, her knowing what he expected the answer to be. Therefore, not allowing him to pose the question of affirmation, "Did I ever tell you that?" She would simply answer Yepper not allowing him to complete a single question of pretentious curiosity. The magnificent wonderment of the whole escape was in her answers, whether she was actually aware or not her answers were and are one hundred percent true. Rudy stated he was not egotistical, that he was only confessing. Pretty well put and I believe that to be an informed impromptu. She said, "Good-bye." Rudy said, "Later!" Then, simultaneously click went the receivers.

Wondering what that evil self-patronizing wench would do next directed Rudy's thoughts while he immersed a tired body into bed. Lying, eyes wide open, his mind racing, having a torrent of simulations in an array of what's next and how he'd handle this predicament of personality sabotage. Not being able to sleep, Rudy would hit the deck early the following morning attempting to list questions pertaining to his predicament. Intentions, directing these questions of unrest to his attorney. Needless to say, hoping for an answer to unravel this Peyton Place provoked by the mephitic hag.

Rudy was and is law abiding, subsequently proceeded in the proper mode of contacting his attorney and relaying to him his plight while attempting to transcend any and all unjust accusation. His attorney at that time attempted to console him to no avail.

He, the attorney, informed Rudy as to what and what not to do, then he requested Rudy to call him later that afternoon. His attorney's reasoning, he would contact the sheriff's office where the alleged accusation had taken place and at which time he would attempt to acquire information informing him if there was merit to information Rudy had presented to him. If so, he at that time would make arrangements as to when, where and how Rudy would post bond along with a dollar figure that would imply the financial significance of such.

Rudy continuing onward with his destination and consequent to arrival completed intended delivery at which time he was scrambling working with dispatch trying to secure a load past the locale he at that time referred to as home. Determination the key factor attributing to success, subsequently Rudy did obtain a load directing him past the house.

His attorney obtained a date of litigation, so Rudy orchestrated a timely arrival. While in the hall of justice and in the presence the magistrate, the charges of allegation were read. In conclusion of read allegations, the impartial (not) so-called judge inquired if Rudy had anything of controversy to dispute. At that time, Rudy presumed there would be no time like the present and not a more opportune time to address the accusations in question. Next, Rudy put forth an effort to explain his actions, at which time the (*demoncrap*) judge lost his temper, a verdict of several days in the county jail was rendered, at which time Rudy's heart almost stopped.

Happenings next show just how unjust a judge can be. The time in the slammer was to be started immediately. The load Rudy was under had to deliver within forty-eight hours. He still had a thousand miles to travel in order to complete his delivery in a timely fashion. At that point, Rudy made his attorney aware of his plight. His attorney then made a request asking the judge that Rudy be allowed to deliver his load at which time he would bounce[16] home to serve his time in the whoosgow![17] The judge granted Rudy his request nevertheless Rudy pronounces his distaste for such self- impressed lowbrow judges. Prior to making the aforementioned request, Rudy tried reasoning with him about the jail time. Plainly, the judge informed Rudy he had heard all of the feeble excuses he was going to hear and if he didn't zip his hole, it would be six months instead of six days! Needless to say, he attained Rudy's undivided attention and zipping it came sooner than later.

What baffles Rudy to day present is why judges can break the law or rules and not have to answer to anyone. By this insinuation, knowledge of an affidavit this particular judge had in his possession. Simply put, he was not supposed to have this particular affidavit. Rudy expressed displeasure with acknowledgment of this and asked to be explained to how this could happen?

---

[16]   *BOUNCE: Trucker terminology meaning to drive somewhere empty having no load.*
[17]   *WHOOSGOW: Slang for jail.*

![Chapter 14]

RELINQUISHING

Rudy's mind was turbulent, similar to river rapids raging and this too would be a stretch or less than an accurate portrayal of one dejected rejected care worn individual. Knowing this and keeping it to mind's center the need of him transcending the blameworthy obstacle, his jezebel wife. It should not be so difficult to understand. He was relentless, driven by the need to succeed as a means to an end. Rising above this Peyton Place that had so unfairly been brought forth. Trudging forward rarely giving ground he was determined, in which case having his mind's eye focused on the journey's end with a glimmer of hope toward the horizon!

A two thousand-mile trip hither and yon, then the uninvited time of detention under lock and key. His manipulated thoughts, acidic, while inflaming his heart, not unlike a stick piercing hot dogs at a weenie roast he strove on. Rudy, having been dealt the lowest of possible blows, including time served for her immorality and infidelities, including the lies Ellen told in abundance.

Arriving back to Tombstone, a town of semblance in nature to his real town, and knowing in a short he'd unwillingly have to go visit Wyatt Earp and be locked up. He wondered if Doc Holliday would be there. These, the thoughts going through his mind, Rudy explained, trying to get ahold of the light side of this undesirable ordeal.

Standing outside the jailhouse on this occasion, at which time included the summing of necessary courage to confront his ordeal. It took major effort stepping through the door. A scarceness of understanding why this out-of- place calamity was taking place but nonetheless relinquished his freedom voluntarily.

Another setting entirely finding Barney Fife not on duty therefore the Barney-et did the honors. Moments noting life isn't fair? Formerly answered conclusively, no it was not and is not. The question challenged preceding jail time. Rudy reinforcing an ever-growing self-pity having an abundance of not- so-lucid waves of judgment being oblivious to why. Embarrassment was intensely difficult. His transportation parked in the jail lot. No one would recognize it for it was borrowed and Rudy was thankful of that fact. Mug shots, what's this? *Me a criminal?* he thought. He hardly thought so and fingerprints too! Why? An elusive answer never to be explained! Like his son had wondered, "How could she do that? Who does she think she is?" His sentiments were kindred to his son. "Who does she think she is?" *Broken hearts. Poor me, poor him*, Rudy thought. "He loved me, I loved him and I'm missing two, too. Finally, he's at peace, then there is me. What about me? I'm now alone and it's tough."

I'm considering a journey to his place of peace, Rudy was weakening! "Caring, who would?" he said. "I'd better stop and think. Know I won't do it. I wouldn't create the chance of making her day." These were the remarks of incoherent thoughts expressed by Rudy. To a degree, his remarks were rather exhausting, so putting forth effort in the needed abundance to grasp the fact was fatiguing. This in mind, I've contemplated the adversity in his mind and I am reasonably sure I've accurately portrayed the points of which he was attempting to project. What goes around comes around. Hers is coming, by the hand of a higher power, this alleviating Rudy for a need of vindictiveness! "Yes!" he yelled. "I'm glad, but still I'm sad. I miss him, oh how I still miss him. Forever a life gone and that day, a day gone. My heart is healing? Yea sure, possible I suppose? Probable? Not too!" Rudy rambled, "Living with no benefit and of course lacking an option don't you know." Rudy spoke of things making sense to him alone, "Dudes in jail, strange rationalizing a fallacy such as it was, quite peculiar, the pair totally harmless and personable." Rudy rambled and rambled on.

"A pretentious accusation and this manipulating a protection order and dilatory child support. Circumstances of yours truly, resembling the former not the latter." Rudy was emphatic pointing out his inmate's problems. Another point of life, of situations and circumstances of fair and it not being! (*Self-admiration of crooks to JUDGES then judges to crooks, relative one to the other and intensely nauseating, falls into this category.*)

While there, the days in bondage another kind of togetherness having an aspect without end. A big deal being locked up it was not Rudy relayed; nevertheless, Rudy should not have been incarcerated.

Reading with much success just wasn't to be but an attempt was made regardless of the results. The disintegration of time in day one was deliberate and very slow thus raising a concern of death by old age before freedom would be achieved. Strange it to be truth and knowledge the center of detour for this hoax of deceit.

Early that evening, Rudy decided to retire. The jailhouse cot comfortless to say the least and would surely give him an appreciation of his own Sealy upon home arrival. Maybe, maybe not, for he hadn't a home.

Disgusting

Thank you to the ex, extracurricular activities such as HEAD[18] together with blood circulation at a minimal, the judge's insight was out of sight. Manipulation a factor once again. He almost overlooked a bit of information and thought you may be interested in this repulsive truism. Yes, she does swallow. Rudy relayed this bit of eloquent wisdom while sporting a smile and simultaneously having a cautious smirk on a care-worn form.

Jailhouse Cot

He lay rationalizing why and how he could land in a life situation so outlandish of intentions and aspirations. Thinking, reflecting of his childhood long ago. Happy yet sad! Rudy implied he was rather small, too small to be small but King Kong hadn't an attitude comparing to him. This quite significant, his attitude that attributed to him overcoming his size disadvantage. Big blue eyes contributed to a nickname Rudy earned not so willingly. It being Rudy Budy, the Blue-Eyed Baby Doll and how he hated that. Falling into a half-conscious state of sleep. Dreaming and remembering he owned up to the fact it

---

¹⁸ *HEAD: Slang for oral sex performed on a male by a female.*

was very difficult in all reality separating and defining drifting sleep and the authenticity of actuality.

Dreaming thinking of her, his first love and not a fairy tale, a live tale of green and hazel eyes having blonde hair. Her smile stopping clocks, any and all. Meeting her, his internal timepiece had lost its tick and tock. The eternal clock of existence she had stopped. Planning a future, theirs, but in all actuality knowing really only his. Therefore, as luck would have it, dreams are what they were or would ever be. In the realm of possibilities, the likelihood that this would come to pass was nil, none or zilch. Years departing so slowly never to return, yet vanishing and he was left wondering where in the hell they had gone?

Drifting in and out of sleep, her kiss rather (*The Kiss*) in the midst of a cold winter but open the door, it's hot, the heat generated from two hearts gripped with a passion. Rudy couldn't breathe and mentally begged to let him go, he wanted out. Then a clatter! "What's that noise, damn it?" he cursed and wished it would stop. Then trying to capture the dream and wondered where he was. A few moments of joy fulfilled with an unattainable goal in reality. His aspirations were alive still, with a chance of hope to be attained. Pointing out the kiss, about a dream, the dream, not to return. Par for the course hanging on to the wonderment of possibilities to be attained with probability not a candidate for success.

Tossing and turning, agitated beyond normal comprehension. Wakening hollering to him, for him. Damn it to hell, another nightmare, my sweet, my heart, in mind out of my head. Apart we were, apart we are. You are, he is a beacon, a light in the night. When dark in light of day, you are, he is "The Light" that guides the way. A part of me now as a part of me then, my love will never end. Thoughts prevalent, hoping to transcend the mental turmoil of you, of him. Hopes, prayers answered not. What is there to do? Loved him, loving you. Speaking to him last, stating I love you, proud of you too, then, relaying similar sentiments, he to me. His ears hearing these last words, the sound of "I love you. Drive careful! If you wreck and were killed, I would die too." His final words, still in his ears, Rudy's story wandered. "Don't worry, I'm cool. Love ya, Dad," then his notable, "Later," his expression of good-bye. "A word I love, it's him, a word I hate. Later was too late, it arrived, never! It never came!" As Rudy told this I was baffled with the emotion that engulfed us both. Especially me, hence the tears that dripped from my eyes as well as his were tears of true love, his, and sympathy, mine. Ironic us being adults and we neither were ashamed for the tears and sobbing.

Rudy daily weighed possibilities of trying to calculate the likelihood of such an abundance of insurmountable grief going south. At this particular time, Rudy not seeing it happening. His luck was only in the mind so no luck was the immediate outlook. He wondered what was there to do. So blue about his son, waiting, wondering, what was in store from the whore, Ellen? Waiting and watching Rudy surmised of possibilities, which would make him glad and alleviating his burden. Not happening any time soon! WAKE UP! What? Oh my god, was Rudy's startled response to the rude bellow to rise and shine. Finally conscious, he inferred it was good to be awake. A dream, nice, then a nightmare. Rudy did not want to let the preceding go, and needing to allow the later to dissolve. Not transpiring any time soon he supposed! Par for the course!

Rising, adorning the jailhouse attire distributed - short of a fashion statement was Rudy's description. He wondered what the day would bring; knowing that hatred and resentment was the captain and first mate of the ship setting sail for the days to come. The breakfast of cold cereal and a banana, what he'd call a desirable meal when in childhood, although he didn't have any complaints. Actually, he liked cold cereal and the banana was a treat, consequently not so bad. The days were long to long so trying to read was what his concentration entailed but being elusive it was futile. The endeavor of reading was to no avail. The inmates sharing the elegant lodging seemed harmless and even likable. The one facing similar accusations as Rudy. The other dilatory child support. He had lost his job and was attempting to solve the matter with a job he had located. With perspective from the present, making no sense having locked him up. Reflection then a question of was it going to help his ex financially, him being locked up? Some judges are so damn stupid it's too bad stupidity is not painful or deadly to rid the earth of such self-impressed pompous ass holes. When the days came to an end, they were requested to retire to their private cells of security at which time they locked them away for the night. Isn't that special?

Rudy described one night, of several nights, having sleepless

<hr>

     Short: Referring to time to be served.

discontent. Rudy's mind working overtime attempting to understand the dilemma facing him. The major participant the primary disputant, Rudy. The duration of this visit was monotonous and cruel. A time of contemplating a next-step action. What to do when released and once again a free man? In and out of sleepless nights, fitful describes the sleep to say the least, trying to dream of blonde hair and those green eyes, love not to come, she being married, so better put that unwholesome notion to the prevailing winds. Time playing tricks, difficult, it being definitely indefinite. Seeming at a minimum was sleep coming in increments that were all too short and comfortable – hardly - he dared to say! Disparity at a maximum suddenly the wakeup call, again!

"Damn it, boy, the cots we were to sleep on were hard on a guy," Rudy implied. A stiffness generated, relative from the injury he had acquired years prior was almost too much to withstand. Jail time he had received, intentions, supposedly to forewarn him of what was to come if he didn't settle down and accept the fact Ellen was nothing short of a conniving, mind manipulating, thieving Manic Depressant. Actually, accomplishing these intentions were in vain. The exact opposite was exhumed reinforcing the hate and contempt directed towards the pretentious jezebel, Rudy enforced.

"One more day of expectation fueled by anticipation, then again I will have my freedom," Rudy expected. He was wondering if Ellen would still claim to be frightened. Her sleep would be anxious but not from fear but from compelling guilt. Knowing her mental state more assuredly than anyone, Rudy said he could affirm she was and is only a New York second away from going completely loony. She was a little wayward anyway. A feeling of compassion for her predicament, Rudy is unable. "The self-serving fancy woman deserves all the feelings of hopelessness she is forsaken with and more. So, Satan do your deal of calamity, standing in your way, I, Rudy, will not. Good luck!" Rudy said.

The day started as any, once again an inspirational breakfast of cereal and a banana. A good breakfast is significant to the start of a good day. "The day was started correctly," Rudy voiced with apprehension. That day following breakfast, Rudy's cellmates were taken out on a work release. He was left alone in confinement. Disliking this opportunity of being alone Rudy did not. A different form of solitary confinement would best describe his predicament.

The scenario of being alone was appealing, consequently a beef he did not have. Only a few more hours experiencing the life of a criminal, then the doors would open standing in wait his freedom. In the meantime cleaning the jail cell, sweeping the floor, scrubbing the postage stamp size shower that was in joint use with the other jailbirds and was not his choice of the moment but a necessary task so Rudy completed it, then the others returned from work release, expressing much joy of being outside, it a welcomed adventure. Rubbing it in a bit because Rudy had remained incarcerated with temporary release not an option. The last laugh was Rudy's when making it abundantly clear that he was short,[12] therefore out of there in another hour, so the teasing adjourned. He hated doing that. But they started it, and he finished it! His dad would have been proud! His dad always said, in dispute, always finish what another starts. It appears that Rudy did finish the verbal squabble with the dignity of being the victor!

The time was now and Rudy's release came and went without incident. A free man again. Yes! Free to go, but where? Rudy took the borrowed car home and his friends transported him to his truck. Made proper safety checks then headed for the nearest truck stop. It was late in the day so Rudy caught a shower and hit the hay.

An appearance of losing the war of who's naughty and who's nice was misleading. Why this assessment? In essence it's simple. Rudy doing time in the county place of incarceration. Known to most as jail. Theatrics along with mind manipulation seem to have won again. Wondering, do you suppose, an illusion may have transpired first and foremost? If so, needless to say, quite misleading?

Boy, it was good to be home. Home? What's this? Actually, Rudy's truck was his home. Not too spacious but covetous, he didn't or doesn't have a driveway and sidewalks to scoop. "That is an advantage, isn't it?" He smiled and said, "I perceive it as so!"

Sleep constantly elusive, restful nights derived exclusively from celestial daydreams, there was none. This direction, seemingly taken without choice. In wonderment of sleepless nights and its conclusion? The days, weeks and months upcoming that would hopefully regard calmness were greedy and covetous. They were not willing to release any feeling of peace in Rudy's direction. Forethought entangled and compensation was evasive. A question, continually plaguing the mind of - WHY?

Working like there was no tomorrow, weeks and months to

come a blur. Paying lawyers plus accrued credit card debt incurred conveniently with devious regard by Ellen. Intent, wreaking havoc in Rudy's direction. Salting cash away with devious intentions nearly working. Rudy managed to pull his cool out of her mismanaged bag of tricks. An accomplishment that he regards as favorable. It was extremely beneficial he supposed. Praise the Lord, small favors are wonderful at times.

Set Free!

Attempting to reach conformity with Ellen, more him than her, so as to finish the divorce. Divorce court, the date being set and postponed several times because of the pitiable Ellen, a time or two by Rudy's attorneys and a couple times by a judge having problems with blood circulation. Kind of odd judges would have the same disability but naturally not for the same reason. ☺

That day, the divorce trial, a half-fast end to turmoil. Completely satisfied, not, getting accustomed to a less than desirable conclusion, not optional. Leading Rudy to believe it could have been worse or possibly duped again. Although suspicious, the ordeal in quest gives a new meaning to being born again. Rudy can start living. He wonders where to begin. Or maybe better how to start over. One thing is for sure, he will reckon with that part of his dilemma.

Apologizing, Rudy digressed saying his trucking had been a necessary means. Consequently, favor or ill fated, it preceded an end of a beginning. Ending a meaningless relationship, sad the relationship, yet glad in the deliverance of freedom from the oppression that had been suppressing him for such a long duration. Unfortunately ending years later than earlier as it should have, which is when the tale of morality should have taken place. Fortunately and finally ending though, better late than never, a cliché spoken with endless validation! Once again, the Lord takes care of kids and fools, thinking idioms as such to be words alone but beginning to see the merit in clichés such as that one. Surely, derived with similar individuals as Rudy in mind! Miles and moving again, blinding, a setting sun!

There was a never-ending blacktop disappearing into the horizon, its boundaries without an end as a final result.

The sun bright was having a semblance akin to the aspirations in Rudy's forethought. His reminiscent regard was of a woman,

Australia, a poetry bash, a persistency in memory equating to Euphoria – then - and later he does presume! ☺!

Rudy woke searching, wondering what was reality and what were images of the mind? This was the end and a beginning:

THE END OF THE END OF A BEGINNING
—AND—
A BEGINNING FOR A NEW END ☺ ☺ ☺ !!!

The End